Tales of Wild Light

by

Stewart Hotston

ISBN: 0995701903
ISBN-13: 978-0995701908

DEDICATION

I would like to thank Benjamin Burroughs for providing space and time, as always, for me to do this in addition to everything else going on. Finally, to Boo and H – your smiles and passion keep me full of joy even if you insisted that Harvey would have been a better film if we had actually seen the rabbit.

TABLE OF CONTENTS

UNMAKE THE WILD LIGHT

Diana sat on the carpet, her hand drifting in a pool of distilled water scented with orchid petals. Her dress ruffed around her folded legs and spilled across the floor all around her, stopping anyone from coming within ten feet of her. Its edges fell, unnoticed, in the water.

Shards of sunlight cut through the hall from windows high in the vaulted ceiling. The water sparkled under their caress, ripples cresting in the wake of her fingers.

For the hundredth time that morning, she thought about her plan: about its consequences, but mostly about the chances of her succeeding. Diana had been born into an ordinary family, except she had seven sisters and her mother was an eighth daughter as well. She always knew she was special.

As far back as she could remember, people would visit the house with the express purpose of seeing her. They would come in their droves, singly and in groups. Whole villages came to the capital, at those times of the year when the wild light was at its weakest ebb and travel was more or less safe.

She couldn't remember when she realised that all they really wanted was to touch her, to look at her; if they could, to have her say a few words of blessing. Her sisters were an intrusive background noise, her aunts an unwelcome buzzing from the periphery of her existence. Her parents, especially her father, would endure days of petty, selfish and even occasionally well-meaning advice from the rest of the family.

Diana wasn't sympathetic. Her father had been a smith, respected but neither wealthy nor influential. Diana loudly wished her mother had married better, but if there was one thing she knew, it was that her father had taken the opportunities her birth had afforded him with both hands and everyone had prospered as a result.

Her aunts might complain about not being listened to – they would definitely gripe at the seating arrangements when important dignitaries came seeking guidance and blessing from the Unmaker – but her father had a look, which stopped them still.

He would place both his hands on the table in front of him, take a deep breath and close his eyes. Even the most insistent of his brothers and sisters-in-law would trail to a halt at his expression of long-suffering restraint. Diana had experienced the volcano beneath his patience more than once as a child and shared their fear. They had moved from a foundry on the corner of a busy thoroughfare near the port to the hills overlooking the bay, where the richest merchants and the most influential nobles lived in their villas. The land around them was sculpted in green, granite and marble.

From the time she could answer people's questions, Diana spent very little of her life at home. Instead, each morning, the Unmaker's Counsel would arrive an hour after sunrise and escort her to the Waiting Hall. Most of her day was spent alone: tradition allowed only an hour, before sunset, for petitioners to come and visit her. They would wait outside from before sunrise, standing under huge umbrellas in case of Lightfall or rain. During the festivals, such as the Celebration of Dark or the autumn equinox, when all marked the ascension of night over day, she would sit and receive pilgrims and visitors from sunrise until sunset. Those times left her weary and irritable. Fat merchants would ask her about trade, make her point to which goods they should buy. Mothers would bring their sons and daughters, asking her to foretell their futures or to tell them to be better behaved. Politicians and nobles would arrive with people they wished to impress, forcing their way to the front of the queues and speaking too loudly so that all might hear their wisdom.

For a while, until she was old enough to suspect she could demand anything she wanted, Diana thought she would never learn to read or write. She taught herself basic numbers, was delighted with herself at being able to count all her fingers and toes. When the first of her tutors arrived, she was embarrassed to discover just how little she really knew.

The first tutor didn't last to the second day; his disgust, when he learned of her ignorance, had him refused entry the next morning.

Regardless of her teachers, Diana took to literature like a starving man to food. Although she was interested in the lives and stories of the Unmakers who had come before her, Diana's real fascination was with whether she was treated with appropriate regard. The earliest histories – scrolls and leatherbound books whose pages were brittle with age – didn't discuss their privileges, except in reference to the ritual of Light and Dark, the Celebration of Dark, and Night's Victory, the winter solstice.

Academics, awkward in ill-fitting suits they hadn't worn since graduation, would deliver the books she asked for, taking any opening to try and explain them to her.

Diana always started these meetings the same way: "I don't want to know about their culture, their lives, their virtues or what made them special." In general, the newer ones deflated, while those more familiar with her brand of calculated indifference would sneer silently and leave her alone, retreating to join her servants at the edge of the hall.

Only one of them ever managed to connect with her, a lecturer by the name of Maedge, who realised the young woman before her was trying to find a benchmark by which to measure herself. Seeing Diana struggle, and latch onto her own sense of privilege, Maedge started bringing modern histories which focussed more closely on concerns she could relate to. She never offered any explanation, but one day simply started pointing to pages and images she thought might please her: "If you turn over, you'll see the dress she wore on the day she went to the Wild Light, a beautiful azure and oyster gown."

Diana didn't respond at first, but after Maedge had left, she found the image of the dress and studied it long and hard. The next time the professor came to see her they played the same game, except that Diana said, "The edges of the dress, what were they?"

Maedge took the book, daring to kneel on Diana's train in order to reach it, and pointed out the lace detailing, explaining how it had been made and why. "This was before we had sewing machines. There was a scandal because it was claimed children weaving the lace went blind."

Diana wondered who would go blind for her, but didn't say anything. Sniffing, she waited for Maedge to finish before taking the book back and flicking through the pages as if the woman hadn't spoken at all.

If her father prospered from her status as the world's Unmaker, he also let it take him away from her. He would appear at festival time, standing in the background and refusing to discuss Diana with the hordes of people clamouring for his time. Her aunts, who were always ready with an opinion, were the only ones to offer explanations for his behaviour: "He loves his money."

"He loves power."

"He is so ungrateful."

Diana tried to ignore them – in this as in everything else – but the constant commentary gradually wormed its way through her thoughtd.

Only her mother defended him. "He loves

you, Diana, and he can't watch what this life is doing to you. People won't even let him provide for you while you're still with us. Don't be angry with him."

Diana didn't understand; her mother may as well have been speaking a foreign language. "Why doesn't he just tell them to stop?" she asked repeatedly, refusing to believe that he couldn't just make it so. "If he really wanted to spend time with me, he would. It's not like he can't afford to stop working for a while."

In this, as in so much else, her mother loved her by not alienating her. She would sit in silence while Diana ranted about the food, or the lack of freedom. She softly spoke of what was happening in the world outside, focussing on people and places Diana knew little about because to talk of family would leave her morose.

Diana's childhood friends had been few, and even those had disappeared from her life long ago, along with her sisters, who, like her father, rarely visited. Their rare visits were full of awkward silences and stilted, resentful conversation. They hated her for the wealth she so dismissively accumulated, while she was driven into furies when they routinely moved from greeting straight into demands for money or intervention in their petty disputes.

Her mother, Saha, was the rock to which she

clung when all else seemed meaningless.

"Your life is the one that matters most," said her mother when she tried to articulate the emptiness she felt inside.

Diana sighed. "I matter because of what will happen *sometime*. Something I didn't ask for."

"We all look forward to that future for you," said Saha, a twinge of her own sadness colouring her tone. "You are the most blessed of all."

"Why doesn't it *feel* like that?" she asked. "Why do I feel like a doll, left in its house until the children want to play? Is my only worth in being used?"

"Certainly not," said her mother fiercely. "You are my daughter, this family loves you."

Diana rolled her eyes.

"We would love you even if you weren't the Unmaker." Saha placed her hands on Diana's and stared into her eyes. "I love you, you are my meaning."

"Part of it," said Diana.

"Yes, part of it. But love isn't finite, my darling. I don't have only so much to pass around. I love all of you, your father, your sisters, as much as I can bear. Sometimes more than I can cope with." She sighed. "When your father is away on business, I can't sleep. I feel like I'm missing a hand."

"You love me like your sisters?" asked Diana, coming out of her funk, a sly grin on her face.

"Of course I do," said Saha before she realised her daughter was teasing her.

The problem with her mother, thought Diana, was that she only underlined the gilded cage she had been stuffed into. Each time she spoke of 'love,' of the sweet ache of missing her father, or how her sisters were growing and having families of their own, the chasm within her only gaped the more. She wondered sometimes if it would eat her up before she had a chance to Unmake. Diana knew she was lonely and, occasionally, she would see herself from outside and realise she could be deeply unpleasant to her well-wishers. At times like this, when she was overcome by self-loathing, she stopped seeing people. As she grew older, those times became more frequent, her bouts of depression deeper.

Towards the end, Saha would sit in the shadows at the edge of the hall, unwelcome, and curse herself for wishing the Wild Light would awaken and make her daughter's life worth living.

#

The capital, Loma, was a great bowl at the centre of an alluvial plain, with a high hub at the centre. The tallest buildings were scattered around its rim, which encircled the hub like a wall. Beyond the rim of the city were its suburbs, modern low-rise buildings and smaller settlements; they had softened the historic city wall that ran along the edge of the foothills, forming a second circuit beyond the rim.

The heart of the city was the black marble temple of Night, within which the Wild Light slumbered from decade to decade. There were no priests, no worshippers of night or day, sun or moon. The temple of Night was a place of fear and distress, built to hide what was within from the people outside.

#

One morning, the many ancient brass and crystal bells that hung within the temple began to peal. The watchers — families whose historic duty was to monitor the slumbering terror within — had read the signs; the Wild Light was stirring.

Diana heard the bells before any messengers reached her. Her heart burned, acid in her chest, and she steeled herself as she believed her predecessors had done for the summons. For the walk to the temple where she would confront and Unmake, keeping the world safe for a little while longer.

A messenger came, at length, and her mother Saha shortly afterwards. They were followed by those of her sisters who were in the city. They tiptoed around her, and Diana realised that only now did they truly believe she was going to die, that her life had been a singular preparation for this moment. Pity for the narrowness of their world welled within her. Her father did not come; to her surprise, his absence still had the power to hurt her.

The first members of the Duke's entourage arrived not long after her sisters. She thought they came to honour her, but then the Duke himself, Arran Kilbride, strode into the room. He had come before, but only at Festival, keeping within the normal bounds of tradition, queuing like everyone else to touch her hand and ask her blessing. Saha had said he was only interested in making a show of it.

Looming over her now, he said, "I hope you are ready. The time is coming."

Diana was confused. "Are we not going now?" she blurted.

For the first time in months, laughter filled the hall, deep and harsh. "No, no. The Light is stirring, but it will be at least a week until it awakens. Have you not bothered to read the histories? I know enough lecturers have come to see you with books they wouldn't let anyone else even touch, let alone read." He stopped laughing and sniffed, looking down his nose at her with an expression she didn't understand. "It doesn't really matter I suppose. The Council of Night will come for you when it is time. We are more grateful than you will ever know. I, personally, want you to know that I am humbled by your sacrifice."

Diana wanted to laugh, then; she could feel in her bones the depth of his insincerity. Instead, she sat in silence and waited for him to leave.

Crowds started to gather before the end of that day and, by the next morning, hundreds of people stood or sat outside, some of whom had stayed overnight. The Council of Night took up position outside the hall, refusing entry to all but her family and those of influence. Diana could hear the noise of the crowd, a tinny susurrus that came and went like a heartbeat.

Diana realised she didn't *want* to die. She watched the Council and understood they were guarding her from the crowd, not keeping her prisoner; and thought maybe she had a chance.

And so she planned how she would leave. She ordered food that wouldn't perish, and demanded that a tent be delivered and erected inside the hall.

She knew the servants were rolling their eyes, and took a bitter satisfaction that their disdain for her made them so easy to fool.

#

Diana pulled her hand from the pool of water, scooped up her bag – in which she had stowed the tent and a few days' food – and left the hall.

The sun was only just peering over the peaks to the east, and she stopped to look at her shadow, streaming away from her in the early morning light. Beneath her, down the steps of the hall, was the great square, filled to overflowing with those who had come to see her walk to the temple and face the Wild Light. There were more people than she had ever seen, packed up against one another, even in sleep. The camp was just beginning to stir, early risers tending to chores or making breakfast breakfast, stragglers who had been celebrating Diana all night.

Smoke rose from the cooling embers of the campfires, giving the crisp dawn air a burnt edge.

The Council weren't paying her any attention; she'd planned to sneak past them, but gave up after a few steps. Diana found herself nonchalantly walking down the steps, the train of her dress cut to a manageable six feet, ragged at the edges after she had inexpertly taken a pair of scissors to it.

At first no one paid her any note, but as she reached the edge of the grand square she glanced over her shoulder, mainly to look at where she had come from. She expected to find Councillors trailing behind her, reaching out to stop her. Instead a trickle of people was slowly wandering in her direction. None of them were openly following her and they stopped when she stared at them. The nearest of them, a young man, only a little older than her, was still in his nightclothes. He was watching her, a look of honest curiosity on his face.

Diana ducked her head and continued walking. She found herself on the Northern Spoke, a wide avenue lined with statues and huge elm trees that ran from the temple to the rim. She knew it from maps; the road could carry eight carriages travelling abreast, only narrowing as it passed beyond the old city and into the suburbs, where it ran in a straight line, brick-surfaced, for another hundred and fifty miles, all the way to the second city of Palatina on the far side of the foothills. A map of the continent showed Loma as a depression from which the ground rose up to the mountains in all directions, as if the very earth had been scooped out by some giant.

She hiked her dress up and strode towards the rim. She kept looking over her shoulder as the crowd grew in her wake. Somehow news of her departure skipped ahead of her: slowly, inexorably, she found the road growing busier before her. It didn't occur to Diana that the traffic might have simply been people on their way to work, or carrying out other chores. In her mind the people around her had only one intention; they wanted to see where she was going.

She crossed the inner circuit, one of the rings that ran around the city, and crossed the spokes that formed the network along which the city's people moved. Stopping to wait for a break in the traffic in front of her, she found people around her moving ahead, halting the bustle, calling to her to cross the road. Part of Diana wondered what they were doing, but a voice in her head reminded her that she was the Unmaker and they were simply doing what was right. She didn't know what to think, but did as they asked and crossed the road. Reaching the other side, she looked to see what people would say and ask next. They looked at her in turn. No one moved until, not knowing what else to do, she decided to keep going, to try and make her plan a reality.

The Councillors caught up with her around midday. They didn't speak or stop her, but took up position around her. At this point all Diana could see was flesh and sky; there were so many people she couldn't even see the tallest building over their heads. The Councillors kept people at a bearable distance, although whether they simply managed to attract more people, she couldn't tell.

They stopped at the rim and people brought her food. They shared what they had with the Councillors, and from nowhere, as they ate, music drifted across the crowd. Diana could hear laughter, raucous screams and shouts, jostling and friendship all around her, and felt moved to tears. The warmth in the people insulated her, but refused to touch her, forcing on her a loneliness so deep she wanted to flee. She gazed at the Councillors, the disciplined distance between them a reflection of her own separation.

A young man stared, seeing her crying. He attempted to come to her, but the Councillors stopped him, gently closing ranks and barring his way with their polearms.

He mouthed something at her; she thought he was asking if she was okay. Diana looked away, overcome, but could hear him remonstrating with the Councillors before he left, pushing his way through the crowd and out of sight.

It was evening by the time Saha found her. The boy returned, and Diana realised she'd forgotten him. He led her mother through the crowd, a pair of Councillors escorting them.

They had walked a shorter distance in the afternoon than they had managed that morning. Diana's feet were sore, and she was embarrassed to realise that everyone else was still reasonably rested, comfortable with the distance they had covered. At sunset they came to rest in a small square. Food was brought from local restaurants – to Diana first, and then to the crowd.

"I was never supposed to walk anywhere," she said to her mother.

"Where are you going?" Saha asked.

"Away," said Diana, having no answer that did not die on her lips.

"Have you even thought about what is happening? The Wild Light is awakening," said her mother desperately.

"What is that to me?" asked Diana flatly. "No one ever asked me about it. No one's ever talked to me to find out how I feel about dying so young."

"What you give to us is life," said Saha. "Without your sacrifice, everyone dies." A rumble passed through the ground beneath their feet, and the crowd went silent, music falling still along with voices and bodies. "It's rising," said Saha, softness in her voice.

"I don't want to do this," said Diana. "There are others like me in the city, I know it." She clenched her fist around a fold of her dress, hoping the feel of taut cloth would stop her tears from starting again.

"What is going on here?" asked a voice she knew without seeing its owner. The sound carried across the crowd, a thin reed against the encompassing silence.

"Father."

At the edge of the perimeter of Councillors her father stood, his dark hair pulled back into a ponytail. He was dressed in a pale lilac toga, over which, draped around his shoulders, was a thick grey cloak. He moved gracefully, more like a dancer than a smith. He squatted down beside Diana before falling back onto his rump with a ragged grunt.

"When they told me you were gone from the hall, I thought to myself you had already gone to meet the light. I told people how proud I was of you." His even gaze nailed Diana to the floor. She suddenly felt so young. "No one laughed at me when the messenger told me you were leaving the city." He sighed. "They didn't have to."

Her heart hardened at his words. "You came to tell me I've embarrassed you? I've made your life difficult? You think *that* will turn me on my heels, have me march back down to face a monster you don't even have a name for?"

"Stade," said Saha, putting her hand on his forearm. Diana saw the gesture and fumed.

"Don't," she barked at Saha. "Stop defending him." She turned her venom on Stade. "You haven't spoken to me properly in a decade. I was *four* when you last touched me. Now? *Now* you come and tell me I've *shamed* you?" She stood up and was suddenly aware of the uncountable people filling the square and its surrounding streets, all for her. She turned and found herself looking down the hill, back towards Loma; as far as the eye could see, people stood in the streets below her, all the way down the hillside. Those nearby were silent, listening to the conversation. She could see their wide eyes, their wonder and fear. They understood her as little as she did them.

More quietly now. "What do you know of me?" she hissed. "What do I know of *you?*" She fell forlornly onto her knees. "I don't even know what I'm saving," she said, utter despair clutching her soul.

"Saha," said her father, "leave us. I must speak with Diana alone."

At the word *alone*, Diana burst into sobs.

"I won't go," said Saha.

"Do as I ask, woman. You know what has to be done," said Stade, pleading more than commanding.

A long silence filled the space between them until, taking her hands from her face, Diana saw her mother at the perimeter, in the arms of the most beloved of her daughters, Adelphi.

"What do you want?" she asked hopelessly. "I know the Councillors will take me by force if they have to. Can't you just leave me to sit here? To dream, if only for a few moments, that I'll see tomorrow's sky?"

"I'm sorry, Diana," said Stade, so quietly she thought she'd not heard him properly. "I should have been here."

"Yes," said Diana, "you should. But you weren't, and you can't undo what you've done. There's nothing you can say now that will make it better. If that's even what you want."

"What I want is tell you why."

"So you can feel better? I don't suppose it matters how *I* feel, does it. I'll be dead before morning."

He sighed again, a deep, hollow breath. In

his voice, she heard her own heart.

"Can I speak?" he asked eventually.

Away, down towards the hub of Loma, there came the thunder of cracking stone. Around them the crowd shifted, the first signs of fear breaking out, preparing to spread uncontrollably. The Councillors stood silent and watched.

He took her silence for permission. "When you were born, we knew what it might mean. I prayed it might not be so, that another child would come to take your place, but they didn't. The geomancers came five days after your birth and showed us the charts, how the skeins of magnetism indicated you would be the one. I didn't know what to say or do. It took me three days to sign the forms handing your future over to the city. To the people."

"Three days," said Diana.

He looked abashed. "If I'd taken any longer, they would have taken you anyway, but sent us into exile for our loyalty. I always had more to think of than just you." He rubbed at his eyes. "Even when all I could think of was you."

She felt a sudden urge to take his hands in hers, but resisted. If he thought a sob story like this was going to warm her, then he was mistaken.

"The city made it clear they owned you,

Diana. The Duke said I shouldn't think of you as mine any more. He said they'd make it worth our while, as if saving everyone's lives weren't enough to convince us."

"So why did you take what they offered?" she asked.

"I couldn't come and see you. I couldn't *look* at you, too young to understand what was to be asked of you. It was easier to walk away, to find something to fill my time, my hours. Providing for my family so that when you were gone they'd not need anything ever again. I won't have my kin in need."

"I don't see why you'd worry," she said bitterly. "You'll still be a businessman tomorrow."

He looked at her, head cocked. "No, I won't."

She rolled her eyes. "Why not? Are you going to face down the Wild Light with me?"

"Yes," he said, simply.

She stammered, not sure she'd heard him right. "Don't be stupid."

"I've always planned for this," he said. "Ever since they took you from me. I might not have been able to be there for you, but I've always looked to this day, my love. I have always meant to walk down the hill with you."

"You can't *do* anything," she said.

"Yes, I can."

"What? Die?" She regretted the words the moment they left her mouth.

"Yes," he said. "You won't be alone. Not for all the time you have left."

"How do you know?" she asked. Did he know what was to come?

"I don't."

A shaft of dirty, writhing light shot up from the hub, followed by a rolling wave of thunder that passed over them and continued on up the hill. The trees at the edge of the square shook, as if they saw what was to come and feared it. Around the beam, clouds collected, swirling and ugly, lightning arcing across their surface. The night was turned to a sickly parody of midday.

"It looks alive," said Diana, her stomach turning over.

"I think we need to go," said Stade. The Councillors had widened the perimeter, two of them coming towards her and her father.

He stood and pulled her to her feet.

Saha watched them from the sidelines, her gaze lit by the Wild Light stretching into the night. She held onto her arms tightly, as if to let go would see her dissolve. Without asking, Diana slipped one hand into her father's and they started to walk down the hill. The mass of humanity opened before her, people clapping, saluting or crying as they passed.

The crowd fell away as they closed with the city. Only the Councillors kept pace, their silver blue armour reflecting the light like the lighthouses on the cliffs of the bay.

Eventually, somewhere between the rim and the inner ring road, they stopped as well, leaving Diana and her father to carry on alone. The light, from this close, pulsed and slid like seaweed in the shallows. It hung in the air, tendrils striking buildings near the temple and destroying them, as the onrushing tide topples and smoothes the sand.

Taking those last steps with Stade, Diana felt a joy rise in her heart and, to her own surprise, a smile breaking across her lips.

WAKE UP SWEET WYRM

Ole sat looking west. It was close to midnight, the sun still clear above the horizon. A hundred yards from him, a party was unfolding, fires dotting the beach. A whole pig sizzled on a spit; it wouldn't be ready until morning. Seaweed drifted along the waters' edge, the curiously timeless dance music the mainland Europeans seemed to love puncturing the indifferent hiss of waves on sand.

A tall, willowy girl with long blond hair tied in a ponytail wandered along the shore in his direction. He'd seen her from a distance during his shifts at the farm. She didn't acknowledge him, but stood a few yards away, facing the sea. Hands in pockets. Her skinny arms were wrapped around her torso; she looked cold.

She was as pleasant to look at as the endless

horizon. He wondered whether she'd have to stand on tiptoes if they kissed.

She knows I'm here, he thought. *What does she want?*

"Hey," he ventured, his voice lost in the ocean's swell.

She turned on one foot, pulling her hair out of the way to look at him over one shoulder. Her legs crossed at the ankle; for a moment, he wanted to leap up and steady her. A weak smile crossed her lips. He smiled back, apparently prompting her to make a decision. She walked over to him and sat, joining him on the sand.

"Hi."

"Ole."

"Brigete," she said, holding her hand out to be shaken. He was surprised to see water on her cheeks.

"Is everything okay?"

She shook her head, but didn't answer.

He turned back to the sea, content to have her beside him, that he was company she'd deliberately sought out. An easterly breeze blew from behind them out to sea.

"You're not Norwegian," she said.

"Half British," said Ole. "I was born here, in Bergen. My mother was English. I grew up in London."

"How come you're here?"

"I was a teacher," he started. He felt her shift, her attention wondering. "I decided to come and travel around Norway for the summer. Work my way around. You know, do a bit of handiwork to pay my way? Wound up here, nowhere left to go."

"You sound lost."

He laughed. "Maybe. Never had anyone to show me where I was supposed to go. My parents died when I was young."

"I heard. What happened to them?"

"My father beat my mum to death." The words burnt as he said them, but he'd spent years forcing himself to face the truth of it. "I was hidden in my bedroom one night. I could hear them arguing. I heard the shouting turn into screams and thuds, followed by a sudden silence. I lost both parents that night."

"They're both dead?"

"No, just my mother, but I've not spoken to

Petar since that night. I'm lost to him. I have every right to feel bitter." He pushed at the sand with his feet. "I'm proud that I don't. My friends have experienced the same life, some worse. When they get drunk on vodka, they go on about just how useless their fathers were. They never talk about it like it's personal; they believe they're stating a fact of life. 'Fathers are of no use, once they'd finished their duty between a woman's legs. Our mothers were better off alone.'"

She listened quietly.

"When I'm sober I'm embarrassed by them. I avoid anyone that lives as though things said through the bottom of a bottle are true under the light of the sun." His toes had found a stone under the beach. He kicked against it with his heel.

"Obviously, I couldn't follow in his footsteps. I became a teacher like my mother, as much to keep her memory alive as to try and find something to do. I convinced myself that I'd make a difference, that the schools I worked in were special. I failed. I handed my notice in at the beginning of the summer and have been here ever since." He didn't say that, at twenty-four, he felt old. Wasted, like a balloon that had deflated before the party had started.

Brigete shuffled closer as the wind blew harder. She laid her head on his shoulder. "My father died today."

Ole didn't know what to say. He put his arm around her instead.

"My whole family. In a car accident."

"I'm sorry."

She pulled her head away. He looked to see her eyes, full of tears, drinking him in, begging him for something he couldn't begin to give. She was so vulnerable then, he wanted to give her strength, to give her the love she'd lost. So he kissed her.

Brigete returned his advance and, as they fell together on the sand, Ole wondered if someone who'd just lost their family believed in love at first sight.

#

Brigete survived her mother and father. Her grandparents were already gone; her only remaining relative was an old uncle she'd not seen since before she started school. She spoke with her uncle on the phone in the days following the night on the beach. Ole had become an almost constant presence in her life. He talked about his parents, his own loss. Brigete clung to his words as to a life raft.

Ole drove Brigete to the funeral in Drammen, the small town southwest of Oslo her family had come from. A few dozen people turned up in the pouring rain, but none stayed afterwards.

They'd said goodbye to the black slab of a priest and were heading back for the car when a heavyset man in an ancient grey leather jacket approached them.

"Brigete?" he called, asking her something in Norwegian that Ole didn't understand.

"This is Ole," said Brigete after a moment.

"Aleks," he said, shaking Ole's hand before grabbing Brigete in a bear hug. "You have been looking after my niece?"

Ole nodded, and the big man smiled, revealing a set of misshapen, nicotine-stained teeth.

"How long have you been in Norway?"

"Six weeks," said Ole. He'd been planning on going home, resigned to teaching in the new term, but since he'd met Brigete thoughts of London had faded into the background.

"You're staying, then." Aleks saw the debate in Ole's eyes.

"Enough, Uncle." Brigete opened the door to the small car. "We're heading back to the farm."

"I can't let you go," said Aleks so firmly that

Ole briefly wondered if they'd be able to outrun him if they had to.

Brigete sighed, then nodded. "Ole, you don't have to come, but it is a family tradition. We sit a wake for the dead."

Ole saw the tiredness in her eyes. He was reminded of his mother, on those nights when his father was recently out of work, with enough money still to get drunk, but with no hope on the horizon. "It's fine," he said. "I'll come."

She looked at him, an expression he couldn't decipher.

"If you want," he continued, awkwardly. "I don't want to intrude."

"Great, that's settled then," said Aleks before she could respond. "I'll get my car, just follow me." He loped away like an excited bear.

They got into Ole's little car to wait. "Why are you coming?" asked Brigete. She sounded dulled. His decision to go with her hadn't hit her as he thought it might.

He shrugged, unwilling to discuss his own family, although his own mother's funeral had been at the front of his mind all afternoon. "Seems pretty lonely to sit a wake." He turned in his seat. "No one should be lonely at a time like this."

Brigete smiled thinly. It was permission at least, if not enthusiasm.

#

The drive to her uncle's house took three hours on narrow, winding roads that clung aspirationally to the sides of mountains. Their route dipped down to tiny bridges spanning fierce white-water rivers, and zig-zagged hundreds of feet up fir-studded hillsides. Aleks led the way, racing ahead with terrifying ease. They'd find him revving his engine at the side of the road after having disappeared out of site, when Ole's own nervous driving had seen his tail lights wink out ahead of them.

"He's bloody mental," said Ole, after Aleks had gone up onto two wheels to round a hairpin bend rather than slow down.

"He lives here, knows these hills like his own face." Brigete was obviously irritated by both of them. Ole was too terrified to worry about her snarkiness; getting to the family farm in one piece was all that concerned him.

The farm was slung against the lee of a towering hillside. Sixty-foot fir trees scored the night sky, their thick trunks hiding the large wooden caravan until the dirt road turned into the driveway. A porch lit by two oil lamps, with solar candles running along each side of the road, drew him in. It looked warm, a safe refuge from cold winters and foolish indiscretions.

The ground was muddy, the boundary unclear, smaller trees crowding in around the property as if they were keen to reclaim the land for themselves. The fixed-base trailer was large for what it was, though still just one storey. A single window was set next to the heavy-framed front door.

Ole wanted to ask about sleeping arrangements, but Brigete was too upset to be troubled with details.

Aleks opened up, welcomed them in. "Make yourself at home." He forgot about Ole moments later, dropping into Norwegian to chat with Brigete. She didn't revert back to English, so Ole was left holding his rucksack in the middle of Alek's small living room like an unwanted child.

On one of the bookcases bracketing the large wood-burning stove he found a collection of books on learning English. He pulled one of the really simple ones down and flicked through the pages.

I'm going to have to learn this shit, he thought. He considered driving back to the farm where he'd been working. Brigete's voice, drifting through from the kitchen, held him as iron filings to a magnet.

He slumped onto a soft, unevenly-stuffed leather couch that had seen better times. Starting at the beginning he used the book in reverse; to learn Norwegian.

A quarter of an hour later Brigete came looking for him. Seeing the book she said, "About time, don't you think? You're twenty-four and don't speak your own father's language."

Petulance nipped at his heels, but he kicked it away. He wanted to be better than his father. "I never needed it before. It certainly wasn't of any use to him."

She sniffed. "It's your heritage, Ole. You should know it."

He looked down at the book.

"I'll help you if you want," she offered.

He smiled. The gesture warmed him, in a way that told him he'd stay for as long as he was welcome.

#

"Do you believe in love at first sight?" Ole and Aleks sat on the edge of a high cliff looking over the North Sea. Somewhere to the southwest lay Scotland.

"I've never given it much thought," said Ole.

"Brigete told me you were there on the beach, the day she found out about the accident." Aleks held a beer up, gesturing at an event he could only imagine. "She said you were there for her, gave her space, like you'd known her for years. She said you were a shape that fit right from the beginning. An ocean for her keel, when she'd expected to be beached."

Aleks' words tightened in his chest. "I don't know. She was there. Crying into the horizon." Ole shrugged.

"So it was an accident?" Aleks sounded sceptical. "You came here, gave up on going home to be with my niece... by chance? I don't know whether to punch you or kneel in respect."

Ole sighed. "She had a sadness about her, like a halo. My mother had the same melancholy, the same sense of loss. I'd been gearing up to go home." He fell silent.

"So you fancied your mum," said Aleks. Ole turned his head, angry, but bit his tongue when he saw the gleam in Aleks' eyes. "Your mum, she was from here?"

"No. My dad."

Hearing something in his tone, Aleks said,

"One of *those* kinds of fathers, huh?"

Ole pulled at a root between his feet until it snapped. "Drunkard. A useless, murderous shit. I spent years wondering if I was to blame, trying to figure out what I'd done wrong, that he hated me so much."

"He didn't hate you."

"Worse, he didn't even think of me. I was the creature at the house where he'd return when he'd run out of money." He could see his father then as some giant, standing in the hallway and pushing Ole away as he tried to cuddle him.

"Are you sure it wasn't yourself you saw in Brigete on the beach?" asked Aleks.

"I felt like I'd seen myself when she talked. It's beautiful here," said Ole, pointing with his now empty beer bottle out to sea. From their vantage point, the ocean was smooth as silk.

Aleks grunted. "How's your Norwege coming along?"

"*Not bad,*" said Ole in Norwegian, which caused Aleks to laugh.

"See, it's your mother tongue. No surprise that you've taken to it. You're coming home at long last."

"My father's tongue." Ole smiled, but Aleks' sentiment sat well with him. Working with Aleks and Brigete over the last few weeks, he'd picked up more than he'd thought possible. He felt a welcome, a comfort in the feel of the sounds on his lips.

He was far from competent, but during the day Brigete and Aleks refused to speak English, in the belief that total immersion would help him. At first he was lost; but soon enough, as they taught him the alphabet, how everything fit together, he was nodding along and even answering. It felt as if his mind caught on fire when they spoke around him. It amazed him to know a different alphabet. Gazing down on the sea below, he felt he could sail to different shores just for knowing the letter Ø.

"Come," said Aleks. "I've something to show you."

Ole followed Aleks back into the forest, away from the cliff's edge. A minute or two later, the older man turned right, making his way slowly back towards the sea. Tugging at a large, low-hanging branch, Ole was surprised to see a pathway leading down from the cliff top, hugging the cliff face on manmade steps. Aleks shouted back up to him but the wind snatched away the words. The sun was sinking, hovering above the horizon, its yellow light bathing them in weak fire.

Ole, distracted by the vista, turned back and found that Aleks had disappeared. He shouted, "Aleks?"

The other man's head appeared as if from within the rock, looking at him with an excited expression.

Aleks had ducked into a tunnel that was utterly invisible from the cliff top. Ole looked out to sea: he guessed it would be just as hard to spot the fissure from a boat as from above.

"How did you find this place?" he asked, once they were both out of the wind.

Aleks didn't reply, instead pulling a small pen torch from his pocket and tossing it to Ole. Ole flinched but caught it. Aleks had his own torch out. "Follow me!"The two of them made their way in to the cave. Ole ran his hands along the wall, feeling natural spurs of stone but seeing that the passageway had also been worked. Straight lines, geometric patterns were repeated, their intricacy growing as they delved deeper. And everywhere a figure eight, or circle.

Ole tried to ask Aleks what they were seeing, but the older man kept moving, as if late for an appointment. The passage curved down and around; their torches were the only light. Ole, who was quickly disoriented, was relieved there were no sudden turns, or passages branching off. Otherwise he feared he might have been stuck down there forever.

Eventually the decline flattened out, the ceiling dropping so they both had to stoop to continue.

"Just a bit further," called Aleks from ahead as Ole found himself contemplating the need to crawl on his hands and knees.

He popped out of the lowest point in the passageway to find himself in a large bell-shaped room whose peak disappeared into darkness above. A long trench ran around the edge of the room, echoing the inscription. Cocking his head to one side Ole saw what the carving was designed to show. "It's a snake! Swallowing its tail."

Aleks laughed, lighting old iron lamps that smelt of burnt caramel as they burned. "Not a snake, a serpent. *The* serpent. The dragon, Jormungandr."

A month before and Ole would have been lost, but in the children's books he'd been using to teach himself Norwegian, he'd read and reread fairy tales about the world snake a hundred times.

Jormungandr, the only dragon that mattered. The obsession – and eventual downfall –

of Thor, the Norse god of thunder. A creature said to encircle the whole world, who would wake at the end of time. He'd skewered the stupidity of the tale: how could the dragon be a child of the god Loki – Thor's brother – but also, somehow, larger than the world?

Aleks, obviously remembering the same conversation, said, "Thor and Jormungandr are related. Fucking families, yeah? No one survives them."

"Why's it here?" asked Ole.

"It's a temple. People would come before going viking to your mother's land. Jormungandr was said to live in the sea of Midgard, so they made offerings to it, asking for safe travels, so they could plunder Europe in peace. The gutter you see would carry blood to please the serpent."

"Why is it always blood?"

Aleks shrugged. "I don't know. It's precious, I guess. They hoped it would be enough to stop the dragon from waking before its time; that it wouldn't get caught on their fishing lines."

Ole wandered across the room, taking in the carvings, the smooth walls and floor. Where the head of the serpent swallowed its own tail, a hole had been bored. The blood would have drained away to some unknown exit, rushing out of the cliff, staining it red and feeding Jormungandr.

"How did you find this place?"

"Our family were once worshippers of the dragon. We were godi – priests. Just a hundred years ago, men would come to us before leaving on the whalers, asking for my great-grandfather's interventions." Aleks sighed. "No one comes now. No one remembers, except us."

"Why do you bother?" Ole's fingers trailed cold against the stone. He felt the power of the place, could understand the hold it exercised, but still wanted to hear the reasons from Aleks directly. Untold lives watched them, sea spray dripping from their faces.

"We keep the dragon from waking. Brigete is the last of the line. Her brother would have been godi after me, but he's dead. His children would have been in line to remain here and serve all mankind."

Ole wanted to laugh but Aleks's voice had dropped to a solemn whisper.

He believes this, he thought, astonished.

"She came home because her family is dead, because there is a need now to consider the future. She must follow in her father's footsteps." Ole waited, knowing Aleks was leading him somewhere. "I wanted you to know. It's going to be important to her in the months ahead, as she figures out what waits for her."

"Does she know I'm down here?"

Aleks shook his head. "If you want to tell her, that's cool." He snapped his fingers, remembering. "You won't be able to read them, but..." He pushed on one of the symbols, a mass of whorls surrounded by interlocking, offset, squares. A piece of wall dropped away, leaving motes of dust in the air. Behind it were hundreds of scrolls, each wrapped in plastic, labelled and catalogued meticulously.

"The library of Jormungandr."

Ole reached out, but Aleks pushed his arm across the entrance.

"You can't touch them. They'll crumble."

Ole stepped back, making no effort to hide his disappointment. "How old are they?"

"Some are at least a thousand years old. Others are a bit more recent. The newest was written by my father, forty years ago." Aleks pressed another symbol and the facade slid back into place. "You'd not be able to read them anyway; they're all in Old Norse. If you think our language is funny, you should see some of their letters."

"Will you teach me?"

"Ah, there's no need for that. I've got the translations at home on computer."

#

Weeks had stretched into months. Ole's Norwegian was good enough that he could understand almost everything Brigete and Aleks talked about. He didn't feel completely confident in joining in, but they forced him to participate.

They had not been back to the cave. Aleks had never mentioned it again, and Ole began to question whether it had happened at all, like a ship glimpsed on the horizon that's gone the next time one looked.

Ole knew that they would wake before him, before six in the morning. Brigete could sneak out of bed without rousing him. So he'd taken to setting his alarm for a few minutes after she'd rise, in order to join them in the woods, where they would light candles and practise what he first thought was Tai Chi.

"Europeans had martial arts too, you know."

"Don't be daft. We were all hacking swords and berserkers." Ole laughed at the idea.

Brigete rolled her eyes. "You don't even

realise how stupid you sound. Who wins when a man with an axe attacks a swordsman?"

"I don't know. Whoever's stronger."

"Rubbish. Strength has nothing to do with it, if you can avoid a grapple. Besides, you should have asked what kind of sword and what kind of axe."

"So how good are you?" Aleks asked casually.

Brigete blushed. "You know I can't fight at all."

"Ah, so pot, kettle, black then."

Ole shut up, knowing he would only irritate her if he continued to ask questions that showed his ignorance. He hadn't known her well enough when they'd arrived to say she'd changed, but if asked, he would have told of how she'd become less patient, more austere. Recently she'd complained that he didn't understand honour or virtue. He didn't mind, he knew she was trying to adjust to the duties Aleks had spoken of, duties from a world whose prime values weren't love and freedom, but duty and honour.

"I'm proud of her," he said to Aleks on one of their walks. "I know it's silly, patronising probably, but I can't help it. She's got a direction I never had. She's lost family only to discover that it gives her a sense of who she is."

"Doesn't make it easier," said Aleks.

"Tell me about it," said Ole. "I mean I wish had something of her drive."

Aleks stopped walking, forcing Ole to pull up as well. "I've wondered why you stayed." He held up his hands to stop Ole from defending himself. "I don't really believe in love at first sight. Yet you've been true to her. I figure it's because you've got similar backgrounds, that you've both lost people. I don't know." He sighed. "Whatever. I'm pleased you did. I don't think she would have found her feet if you hadn't been here for her. She's wrapped up in something she's not even sure she wants, but you've been her rock."

Ole never mentioned to Brigete that they'd visited the cave. He concluded the right time would present itself one day but until then he'd use the insight he'd been offered to help her adjust.

One afternoon, after their daily tour of the boundary fences was complete, Aleks drove off to Bergen for supplies. It was the first time in a week that they'd been properly alone in the trailer.

Ole hadn't bothered to wear underpants, too excited to think about what might actually happen but determined to be prepared. He thought it might turn Brigete on to know he'd been looking forward to being with her. Instead, almost as soon as Aleks had driven away, she excused herself for a walk, making it clear she wanted to be alone.

Ole, disappointed, picked up a new book on Norse beliefs. He found the passage he was looking for on Jormungandr. Where Thor, trying to provoke the fates, seeks out the dragon with the aid of one of the giants and is only saved by the giant's intervention. The translation was a hundred years old, but the poetry in the story was handled beautifully.

Except, thought Ole, *that Thor is a wanker.* First he demands that his friend, a giant who's minding his own business, provide bait. When the giant prudently declines, the tosser kills his best cow and uses its head. The poem doesn't record the giant's response to that, except to say that he agrees to take Thor out on his boat. Then, even after he's caught two whales, he insists on going deeper to find and wake Jormungandr.

He flipped back to the start of the story. Reading it again to confirm his theories. *Thor was a prick.* The giant wasn't evil, and even Thor at his most dickish wants to understand his fate. *Christianity has infected my idea of dragons,* thought Ole. *Jormungandr isn't evil either. It's not a devil waiting to pounce, it's just a force of the*

51

natural world. It's Thor who's the problem.

He wrote in his journal, *Thor is the anger of humanity. All Asgard is a reflection of Norse, hence big-man, virtues and vices. Are these poems a way of saying that the end of the world is inevitably bad because, fundamentally, people are arseholes?*

"What are you doing?" asked Brigete, who had come in while he was absorbed in the lunacy of Norse gods. He explained his ideas about Thor to her, feeling increasingly uncomfortable as she sat, face blank, while he talked.

When he was done she snorted.

"What do you think?" he ventured.

"It's all fucking nonsense. There are no gods, no dragon that swallows its own tail."

He laughed politely. "People worshipped it, though, right?"

Brigete frowned. "People thought it encircled the world and lived in the sea at the same time." She laid heavy emphasis on the last four words, sarcasm dripping from her mouth. "They said it would wake at Ragnarok, but it was very awake when Thor caught it on his fucking fishing rod."

"Those poems were written at different times, I guess."

She sneered. "So what? I read one document that suggested the world-encircling dragon live on the Shetland islands, that the only reason the Jarlshof was built there was to facilitate them keeping it asleep."

"The Jarlshof?"

"Oh, it's a ruin on the main island that's been there for thousands of years. Predates the Vikings, but no one mentions that bit."

"Have you ever been?" he asked.

She nodded, softening. "It's amazing, to stand there and know a hundred generations of people came before me, their feet stood there, seeing the same views, the same sky. You can almost feel their shadows carrying on with their lives, overlapping ours as if we were the shades, not them." It was the most alive he'd seen her in weeks.

"Why don't we head into Bergen? Have some time away from here."

Brigete eyed him sadly. "I can't. I'm sorry."

"Just the afternoon." He smiled, "Aleks doesn't have to know." He reached for her arm, thinking it was a good idea he'd not worn pants after all.

To his surprise, she pulled away, her eyes full

of despair. "I have to stay here, that's the end of it."

"So…" he said. "We're all alone here. First time in ages."

She laughed. "Don't get your hopes up."

Ole was deflating, but determined to bring Brigete out of herself. "C'mon, where's the harm? You know he won't be back for hours. Even at my best that's a stretch!"

She traced her fingertips down his arm, eyes averted, thinking. He saw her about to say *no* again. "You drive me crazy. Just smelling you in the mornings gets me hard. Then I remember Aleks is ten feet away. Let's live today!"

She put her hand between his legs. "Oh." She laughed again, with the warmth that always made his heart leap. "I see."

"Easy access." He couldn't help smirking.

He put his hand on her chin, drew it slowly down her neck and onto her breast. She didn't stop him, just closed her eyes.

#

"I shouldn't have let you persuade me," she said after they were done.

"Felt pretty right to me," said Ole, nuzzling

her neck.

She sat up, forcing him to roll away. "I'm not supposed to." She stopped talking, like she'd been slapped.

"Not supposed to? Says who? Last time I checked, you're a grown woman." Ole sat up too, pulling on a t-shirt to stave off the cold.

She looked away, staring out of the window.

"Talk to me," pleaded Ole.

"You wouldn't understand." Her voice was bitter, the first time he'd heard anything like it from her.

"Try me. I might surprise you with what I know." He gently put his hand on her back.

She stilled under his touch. She remained silent for a long time. Eventually, she said, "He told you, didn't he." She wasn't asking him a question. "Bastard. Did he take you down to the temple, on one of those walks you two are always on?"

Ole nodded, feeling the ground open up beneath him. "Yes. It's amazing."

"It's shit," snapped Brigete. She half turned to look at Ole, thinking. "You haven't been out that way for ages. How long have you known?"

Ole leant back from her, uncomfortable.

"How long?" She ground the words out between clenched teeth.

"He never told me you have to be celibate. He just showed me the scrolls."

"I asked you how long?"

Ole looked away, unable to meet her eyes.

"You shit. How could you keep this from me?" She stood up. He tried not to look at her naked body. "You knew I was the last of them, that the responsibility for keeping Jormungandr asleep has fallen to me, and yet you kept sleeping with me."

"I didn't know."

She folded her arms under her breasts. Seeing she was cold, he threw her a jumper from where it lay on the floor. She pulled it on, stretching it down as far as it would go to cover the top of her legs. "Aleks has a sword in his chest that, if stabbed into the dragon, would wake it. He swears he saw the beast's scales when we visited Shetland when I was a child, that my father showed him how to make the creature visible."

"It's nonsense, though, right? You said it yourself."

She sighed. "Yes. It is."

"So why do you care?"

Brigete started to cry. "This is all I have left of them, Ole. If I stop this, this way of remembering them, they'll be truly gone. I'll be alone."

"I'm here," said Ole. distance gulf yawned between them, which he could do nothing to bridge.

"I know." She sat back on the bed, beckoned him to come closer. "You've made my life continue when all I wanted was for it to end."

He wiped a tear away from her cheek.

"I love you," she said, "but you can't be my everything, Ole. You aren't even Norwegian."

"What's that got to do with it?"

"Don't you see, my love? I can only have children with someone who's properly from here. Otherwise, they won't be able to carry out their duties."

Ole couldn't believe what he was hearing. "I'm not Norwegian enough for you? Children? What the hell are you talking about?"

"I'm not racist, if that's what you mean."

"I'm not racist, except I can't have children with someone who's only half-Norwegian as they're not pure enough for me!" Ole couldn't keep the bile from his voice. "I'm also not a father, I just keep having children."

"I didn't ask for this. I love you, but being a godi is more important than love. I hate it, but it's true."

"I didn't ask for this either."

"Yes, you did. If you've changed your mind, then go. I never asked you to come with me, Ole. That was all you."

Ole thought about where else in the caravan he might go. It was simply too small to skulk off into, and he wasn't about to go outside. He had nowhere else to go.

"Fine then, I'll go." Brigete had started to cry, the tears tipping over clenched jaws as she tried to hide them. She pulled on some jeans, grabbing at her socks and shoes when they were buttoned up.

Ole followed her out into the living room, hazily wondering what she was thinking.

She didn't explain herself. The door slammed shut behind her. Ole stood at the entrance. He heard his car start up and drive away.

#

"Where's Brigete?" asked Aleks when he came back later that afternoon.

"She wanted some time out," said Ole blandly.

"You guys need some time kicking back," said Aleks. "I'm not surprised you're fighting. Cooped up here in this tiny shack."

Ole was surprised. "She said she couldn't leave. Wasn't *allowed* to leave."

"Hey buddy, don't look at me. I'm not the boss of her."

"That makes two of us."

"Don't give up on her, Ole. You've kept her sane these past few months."

Ole didn't respond.

"Cheer up. Why don't you two take off for the weekend when she gets back? I can look after things while you're gone."

"She said you'd seen Jormungandr when she was a child."

Aleks drew himself up. "She did, did she? I'm not sure what I saw. A ghost the size of the world, scales as big as cars. A mist that obscured even those around me, as if the dragon was more real than the people stood next to me."

"How?"

"A pair of glasses made from volcanic glass. My uncle said they were made from the dragon's scales, but I had them tested. Blue obsidian."

"If the glasses were fake, then..."

"I know, right? I've tried them on in a dozen places but only there, in the Jarlshof, did I see anything strange. I can't explain it, Ole, but I swear it was true."

#

Brigete returned after nightfall. If Ole thought they'd be a happy family again, he was mistaken. As soon as she saw Aleks, she attacked him.

"How dare you tell Ole about my family!" she shouted.

Aleks wasn't having any of it. "*Your* family? You mean *our* family? I have every right. He's been good to you, he had a right to know."

"Who gave you the right to decide?"

"I did."

Ole, trapped between the two of them, could not let it rest. "I stayed, Brigete. That's all that matters. I stayed then and I'll stay now. I love you, if anything were to happen to you it would destroy me. It doesn't matter what your Uncle did or didn't do."

"Shut up, Ole," said Brigete, her voice tender but uncompromising.

Aleks said nothing. In silence, Ole took his coat and keys and left. The sun hadn't set, and right at that moment, he had an overwhelming desire to see something beautiful. *The sea,* he thought, dismissing thoughts of dragons sleeping beneath the waves.

#

He noticed the smudge above the trees as he walked the path along the firebreak. At first he thought it was low cloud, but he saw it move in front of the stars and realise it was much closer.

Smoke? It was smeared across too much of the sky to be the wood-burning stove, and too black to be a forest fire. He ran, fear vomiting up from inside, driving him back to the trailer. The roar of the flames reached him before he broke through the tree line. The trailer was in ruins, the roof collapsed, the windows gone. Flames ate hungrily at the walls.

Ole searched for signs that Brigete or Aleks had escaped, but both cars sat on the drive. The paint on Aleks' car bubbled in the heat.

They were ten miles from the nearest village. He had no idea where the nearest fire station would be.

It's all too late anyway. They'd been inside, his heart told him that for certain. He went and sat in his car, hands on the steering wheel, undecided as to whether he should just leave. The flames burned all night.

Ole woke to whited-out windows. Ash covered everything, although the flames were gone. He kicked through the ruins; the embers were still glowing red in the white morning light. A few timbers along the back wall were standing, but everything else was cinders.

Ole found a scrap of Aleks' red winter jacket, a sliver of material with the zip fastener still attached. He couldn't bring himself to look harder.

In the middle of it all was Aleks's chest. The timbers were unharmed by the fire, although a dirty pool of metal was all that remained of the lock. Ole approached hesitantly; he caught himself checking to see if anyone was looking.

The lid rose easily. Within he found a stash

of cash, along with a sheaf of bank statements. It seemed Brigete's uncle was a very rich man.

Not that that's any use to me.

Underneath the statements were robes like a druid might wear. He lifted them out, his fingers staining them with soot. Then he saw the sword, only a couple of feet long but viciously sharp. Folded next to them were the glasses, the lenses dull blue lenses and faceted.

Jormungandr came to mind. *If she's gone, then it doesn't matter anymore.* He picked up the glasses and sword, careful not to catch his hand on the edges.

As he drove away, he had only one thought: Shetland.

#

The ferry docked to the sound of metal on granite. A thousand screeching seagulls wheeled overhead. A hundred or so people disembarked; Ole hid himself among them, sword and glasses safely packed in a large rucksack he'd bought with Aleks' cash before leaving Norway.

No-one could know what he was in Shetland for, but still he expected a hand on his arm, a challenge, opposition, at any moment.

Finding the Jarlshof was easy enough; the island had built its Sumburgh Airport next door, and a major road ran around and past the ancient settlement.

Having booked himself on an official tour, Ole was surprised at just how large the ruins were. Halfway through the tour, gazing southwest, he could understand why they'd built there. The voe below them, fresh water springs nearby and fertile soil all around. The basics were covered, which for most of man's time on the planet were hard to come by. An oceanic oasis, a bridge between the land and the sea.

Ole lingered after the tour had finished. He hadn't dared use the glasses while they were being taken around. He was confident the story of how to wake Jormungandr was unknown beyond Brigete and her uncle, but he wasn't going to take any chances.

The public was allowed to walk freely along marked paths winding around the site. In the hour between tours he made his way back to the Norse ruins. He recalled Brigete's awe when she stood among them, the sense that others had lived their lives, dreamed their dreams right where he now stood. He put the glasses on, and the world turned turquoise. Nothing else happened.

Doubt gnawed at him. *They're just glasses,*

he told himself. There were no dragons, no prickish gods waiting to kill them. He moved from one house to the next. Each time, nothing. By the end, he'd mostly forgotten he was wearing the lenses. He was going to have to face Brigete's death in full, with no way out.

He was far enough along the path that he decided to walk all the way to the beginning rather than turn back. As he walked he heard a soft murmuring, as of people on the other side of a wall speaking. He stopped and concentrated, but it faded away.

"Hello?" he called, but there was no answer. He waited a few moments in silence before moving on, but soon as he moved the sound resumed, growing louder as he approached the most ancient part of Jarlshof, where people had lived nearly four and a half millennia ago.

The murmur grew into muttering, half-heard discussions, sparks of syllables grasped amongst muted words. The wind picked up, pushing past as if determined to touch him. He swore he felt fingers on his shoulder and whipped around, to find himself alone on the pathway. He looked down; his shadow moved around him like it belonged to another. Holding his breath, he stepped backwards. His shadow followed like it should, but it held a sword where his hands were empty.

An urge to run pooled in his stomach, coiled like a snake. He felt like he'd swallowed an ice cube, the chill unbearable as it needled its way through his chest.

He took the glasses off and everything stopped, except the sense of dread. He looked at the glasses as if they'd betrayed him, turned them over and over. Eventually he put them back on.

A rush of sensation. The negatives of people moving around him, through him. He twirled, trying to find a space through which the shadows didn't pass. There was nowhere to go.

Beneath all of it he could hear a deep rumbling, like the purr of a massive beast.

Jormungandr.

It took a few minutes of searching before he felt confident he had the direction right. The purr grew in volume, deepening, slowing, as if coming from some deeper cavity.

Ole found himself in a small round house, half buried in the landscape. The stones the builders had used were small, smooth, tightly fit together. The impression was of density, a gravity in the earth itself.

The ground was smooth under foot. He saw iridescence shiver across the earth, faint, barely visible. He took the glasses off and daylight poured in, revealing the ruins of a bronze age round house, the ceiling long gone. Grass pushed up from the packed earth in a small arc where the sun reached it each day.

He dropped his rucksack to the ground, pulled out the sword. The blade hummed in his hand, an eagerness seizing his arm, its purpose so close. Ole stood there, the scales of the world dragon under him, Brigete's sword in his hand.

He raised the sword and the whispers ceased. Even the sea's constant static fell away. His first blow was half-hearted, the tip skittering off the ground, a sharp scratch scoring its path. He released the breath he'd been holding.

Raising the sword again, he knew he needed to want an end, really *want* to wake the wyrm. He thought of Brigete, dead in the trailer. It was enough.

"Ole." He looked up, surprised. Brigete stared down at him from the pathway. "What are you doing?"

Suddenly he didn't know. Moments before his course had seemed obvious, but his reason had been undone.

"You're alive?" He took the lenses from the

bridge of his nose, half-expecting her to disappear.

"Of course I'm alive. What are you doing?"

"I thought you were dead!"

She sighed, as if betrayed. "You didn't wait to find out, did you?"

"No."

"You took the only working car and fled. I thought you'd gone to get help, but you never came back."

"I was there all night and the next morning. Where were you?"

She shrugged, jumped down into the roundhouse with Ole. "I argued with Aleks. The sod should never have told you." She pursed her lips. "But he did, and I understand why. I didn't start the fire. I went down to the temple, spent the night. I needed to think."

"What did you think about?"

"Us, me. Our parents. Mine weren't sugar and light either. My father was distant, cold. He thought being a priest was more important than everything. My mother was found for him, by others who shared his faith. To say they didn't love each other would be an understatement."

Ole was filled with hope. "I'm sorry," he said. "I was desolate, lost."

"I made some decisions down there, while you were driving off to end the world." She put one hand on his arm. "I decided, that if you wanted, I'd ignore that bit about having to be a racist."

"You're going to be a priest, though?"

She nodded, her expression crumpling. "I have to. I'm the last one left. My father taught me: if not for us, Jormungandr could be woken before its time. You've stood here, seen it for yourself. Gods, you even fucking *tried*." Her eyes were ashen in the shadowed light of the ruins. "It was his task and now it's mine. It's as much a part of me as my DNA."

The sword felt uncomfortable, suddenly heavy.

"You should give me that." Brigete held out her free hand.

Ole carefully handed the sword over. "Thanks." He felt embarrassed.

"I thought you'd refuse," she said.

"Why would I do that?" he asked, confused. "You're alive."

Brigete held the blade up, examining it in the

scarce sunlight. Seemingly satisfied, she turned with a twist of her feet, one hand still on his arm, and plunged the blade into his stomach.

Ole gasped, blood flecking his lips. Brigete pulled the sword free before plunging it again into his tottering body, this time through his chest, the blade flat, sliding between ribs, into lungs.

Ole fell, pulling himself free, and landed face down, tasting blood and dirt on his tongue. His chest hurt, he couldn't breathe. A boot under his body lifted him up and rolled him over.

"Ole. Maybe now you see."

He couldn't answer.

A tear fell onto his face. "I'm so sorry, my love. Without you, I would never have remembered what my father taught me to be. I'm the last godi of Jormungandr."

He groaned as the last of the air left his lungs, her voice becoming ever more distant, more torn. "I was born to stop Jormungandr being woken. Anyone who might try it is my enemy. Even you." She turned away, sobbing, lost to his dying sight. Ole felt Jormungandr grumble contentedly beneath him, his blood an adequate sacrifice to the world dragon.

BOGGART HILL

"He won't sleep," she said, pointing at the small boy sat under the kitchen table, playing with a wooden train set. The mother, Bev, was a short, sad-looking woman between thirty and forty. Her eyes echoed with hope surrendered.

The kitchen smelled of cooling bread, going some way to counter the persistent chill from the rain-blurred windows. A golden pocket of warmth amidst nature's sallow indifference. The child, her only one, had a ruff of mousy brown hair and dark rings around his eyes.

Stephen had asked the normal questions of the referrer: was the home a happy one, what were the chances the boy was being physically or sexually abused? It was possible that nonhuman inhabitants would instigate or take advantage of an abusive atmosphere, but in his experience the vast majority of abuse was initiated, enacted and fostered by the families themselves. There wasn't any need to look for outside influences. The concept of 'stranger danger' was one fit only for newspapers; the abused nearly always knew and trusted their abusers.

The referrer, a member of a large network he'd once been a part of himself, had insisted the family was normal, caring and loving. Stephen knew his perception of families was skewed by those he dealt with on a daily basis, but in his opinion, the terms 'normal' and 'loving' were mutually exclusive.

Currently he was leant against the edge of the family's kitchen sink, watching Harry silently push a small blue train around a track weaving between the thin wooden chair legs. Harry's mother was warming a pot of tea on the range. Her husband was out in the fields, working herbicide over his winter wheat crop. He'd been gone since five am, and wouldn't be back until dinner.

Bev had promised he would pop in to say hello if he managed to finish up.

"I'm sorry you missed him at lunch time," she said, sounding apologetic for having eaten. Stephen shrugged; he hadn't arrived until two and didn't want to discuss the etiquette of waiting for a guest who had no firm arrival time.

"I'm glad you didn't wait," he said, "My little Renie almost didn't make it." He had a small runabout, perfect for the city but, as it turned out, uncomfortable and unreliable on long journeys. He winced as he thought about the return journey, picturing the misery of a breakdown on the M6, but he turned away from it.

He had a full file on what the referrer believed was going on, but preferred hearing first hand. Bev passed him a cup of tea and sat down at the table with her own, lost in thought and turning the delicate china cup in her hands. He noted that Harry was left playing peacefully under the table; most people tried to shield their children from topics they themselves were uneasy about.

"The chapel up on the hill," she eventually started, "St Cuthbert's, has been locked up these ninety years. No one goes there; it's not somewhere anyone likes. Two months ago, near enough, some preachers came up while visiting Appleby. Local pastor brought them, friend of ours he was."

"Was?" asked Stephen.

"He passed last month. Tragic for his family, it is." She glanced down at her son, indicating that there was a story here she wasn't prepared to tell in front of him. "We'd been fair terrorised until then –

things moving of their own accord, Harry hardly sleeping, the animals uneasy near the house." She shrugged. "The worst were the smells: rotten eggs and dead birds. They'd come through the house like a window was open, leave us without an appetite. The dogs would bark at odd times, never any intruders or vermin to provoke 'em, neither. We didn't like it here, but it's our home and we've a livelihood to keep. This farm is John's family's, and we en't leaving."

"The Pastor, Marcus, tells us the week before they were coming. He says that he'd like to bring them up to us here. We don't have time to go down to the town and see them, and besides, problem's here, not there. They come up and there's three of 'em, youngest is the one I remember most. He was brown, like milk chocolate, but spoke English like he was the queen. Educated, I guess, from the big city. They come in and say there's something here. Even John takes notice of that, because these types normally come and look at us, pray and leave. This brown one, he had an English name that I don't remember, but he talks to us, asks us about our lives and our farm. Says that Harry can see them." She stood and walked to the window by the back door. "We didn't tell him that, he just knew." Bev turned around and looked at Stephen. "I would have done whatever he asked of me, then."

"What did he ask of you?" said Stephen.

"He asked if there was an old chapel nearby, said that he felt they should go up there and pray." She put the empty cup on the work surface and pulled the bottom of her jumper lower around her waist, fidgeting. "We went up, unlocked the place. Prayed and even had a merry sing song. Whole farm seemed lighter for it."

"Then what?"

"We came back down. Joyous, to be honest. Except that when we got back into the house, it was like some old trout had died and been buried beneath the floor. The place reeked. Our man, well he looked lost, not knowing what to do next. It was then that Harry ran through the kitchen, fell and cut clean through his calf. Blood everywhere, screams and shock. The preachers looked at each other and at me as if they were kicked in the face by a horse." She looked tired. "they had the decency to wait until Harry was calmed, but there was no way he could avoid a trip down to A&E in Penrith. We went our ways, then; they were gone back to their own homes by the same time the next day. The one who knew us, he said we should keep praying, keep standing firm." Bev folded her arms. "I'm not a woman of God, I don't know even what that means." She wasn't angry, even if he was. Stephen saw the lines around her eyes, the long fingerprint of fear, the shadow of living with one's head permanently ducked.

"What happened then?" he asked, looking around at the grey stone walls, jaundiced in the kitchen light. Stephen couldn't see anything in the room, but he already knew where he had to go.

"Lights turn themselves off; Harry comes into us in the night, complaining of monsters in the house. More accidents." For the first time Stephen noticed her frustration. "Nothing serious," she said, as if that was the worst thing about it. "Falling lamps, shattered glasses, lost keys. It's like a child having a tantrum."

Stephen couldn't help but glance in Harry's direction.

"It's not him," said Bev fiercely. "The cat won't come in the house, won't even cross the cattle grid from the river side. The bugger lost an ear to a fox, absolutely fearless he is, and now he won't come on our land. He sits there mewling, as if he's trying to get us to join him."

"Harry," said Stephen, his locked eyes on Bev, "could I talk to you about the monsters?"

The train paused momentarily in its journey between the chairs.

"Harry," said Bev lightly, "Come up, I need a

cuddle."

Harry slowly emerged from under the table and climbed up onto his mother's lap.

"I love you mummy," he said.

"I love you too." She ruffled his hair. "Stephen has come to see us about the monster."

The boy looked at Stephen and what he saw made his soul tremble. Harry was stained with corruption. Now that Stephen could take it in, he saw the unmistakable glimmer of haunting, the imprint of something *other*.

He was worried about what the Christians had done. The way the mother talked about the leader, as someone who *knew* her, left him certain the man had been a Seer, literally someone who could see what there was to see. If the Seer had known what was happening here and but had still left, then it worried him. The lingering residue of haunting on Harry felt like something minor, but what Bev was telling him was rare. Very rare, in his experience.

He was sure it had been this way for as long as mankind had been coming together to achieve more than it could apart. Spirits typically clustered around influential humans. Stephen didn't think it was rude to say that Bev and her family were hardly important in the scheme of things and shouldn't have attracted any attention, but some of them had a sense of foreboding – the smarter ones, if they could be called 'smart,' were superb at probability and could sense the potential lines of a person's life. Where individuals were probably going to be in the right place at the right time to change the course of history, too often they attracted powers and authorities, like bees to honey. Stephen did not have that gift of foreseeing, something for which he was very grateful; he had met one or two foreseers in his time, and they were as mental as could be imagined without being functionally disabled.

"Harry," said Stephen, "what does the monster look like? Is he big and hairy?"

Harry met Stephen's gaze and shook his head slightly.

"Is he small?"

Harry nodded. "He's bald, like the man on *Star Trek*."

"Patrick Stewart," said Bev, smiling.

"Does he live in your room?"

"No," said Harry, slowly overcoming his uncertainty, "he lives in the church on the hill."

"Ha," said Stephen; his gut feeling had been

right. "So he comes down here at night-time and frightens you?"

Harry shook his head again, slipped off Bev's lap, and before she could catch him had run out of the room.

"Sorry," she said. "He says the creature sits on his windowsill, or comes in here." She looked around the kitchen as if to confirm its presence. "Harry says it drinks the milk, unpasteurised only. Spills the pasteurised stuff on the floor. We got through four pints one weekend, we weren't even here for most of it."

"You'd gone away?" asked Stephen.

Bev gave him a look he figured was reserved for city types. "We don't get away much, farming's not a job that stops at five on a Friday." She smiled, softening the blow. "Harvest festival. It's always been important for those of us whose lives depend on what we pull out of the ground."

"I guess I know what you're trying to say," said Stephen. "No one was here who could have drunk the milk."

"So what do you think?" asked Bev.

He scratched at the stubble on his chin. "I think I need to see the chapel."

"I can walk up with you after John comes back."

"It's okay, just point me in the right direction and I'll find it eventually. It's not like there are a hundred of them around here, is it?" He laughed, but it was swallowed by the room.

"I'll have Harry walk you over," said Bev, standing and walking to the large door. She shouted for her son to come back, then repeated herself after a few seconds; at length the boy tumbled into the room, a ball of energy. "He needs to get outside anyway."

Stephen glanced out of the window at the rain still drowning the landscape. Any normal mother would want her son inside on a day like today, but then again, he reflected, he didn't know anyone who lived in the countryside. On the evidence so far, their lives were lived to a different rhythm.

He'd have stories to tell when he got home.

Harry came in to the kitchen with a thick winter coat already on and waited for Stephen. The walk to St Cuthbert's took the better part of half an hour, and the path was barely visible. If Harry hadn't been leading him, Stephen would have been well and truly lost. They climbed far above the tops of the farm buildings, towards the fells that cut the country in half, and the clouds hung low around them like fog, shrinking their world. The only sounds Stephen could hear were their footsteps on the frost-shattered rock, and his own laboured breathing. The swish of his coat was as loud as a jumbo jet.

St Cuthbert's emerged from the flat grey air, the last vestige of civilisation before the desolation of the fells. A single, stunted oak tree stood by the southern wall, its forlorn branches scratching the leaded windows.

The building was a single story of light grey stone with a small steeple. A dark slate roof lay heavily on the walls.

Stephen stopped and read the building – it was lonely, that much was obvious, but beneath it he could feel an import, an authority far more substantial than he'd expect from a place as out-of-the-way as the farm. He guessed the farm the old chapel served had once needed many more workers; before mechanisation eliminated their jobs and forced them into the cities.

A hint of shadow along the roof line was gone when he turned to look at it.

"Is this where the monster lives?"

Harry nodded.

Standing before the unadorned wooden doors, Stephen ran his hands over the stone, the grainy, lichen-covered blocks rough beneath his fingers. The doors were new, the windows were clean and the lime mortar was fresh. He was surprised to find the church was so well-kept.

"We look after our history," said a voice behind him.

Stephen jumped. A few feet away stood a thick man with a patchy beard and arms that looked like they could snap him in half, his edges blurred by the softness of the clouds that surrounded them.

"...John?" asked Stephen hesitantly.

"Aye," said John, "Cuthbert's is my family's. My ma and pa got married there, so did my grandfather. Wouldn't be right to let it fall to wrack and ruin."

"You look after it?" asked Stephen, regretting his expression of disbelief almost as soon as he said it. Where he lived, it was inconceivable that anyone would do their own building work.

"Ain't no one else going to do it is there?" said John. "You seeing to the man?" he asked Harry. The boy nodded. Some hidden communication passed between them, leaving Stephen on the sidelines, remembering how he had felt as a small boy talking to his own father.

"You need anything, then send Harry to come get me." John nodded at Stephen and trudged down the path. "I'm down with the sheep in the far field, Harry."

Stephen watched him until he was swallowed by the clouds, suddenly remembering that he was cold and wet. "Harry, can we get in?"

"Yes," said Harry, setting his hand on a simple cast iron ring on the door. He pushed, and the doors swung open without a sound.

Stephen hurried inside, to find half a dozen rows of beech pews carved in a Methodist style, along with a baptismal font and a modest pulpit, raised just a foot from the ground. Thin watery light from the windows left the building feeling cold and hollow. The walls were whitewashed stone.

Stephen took a breath; the air was dry. John clearly took pride in the place. Beneath the sterility of the interior Stephen could feel the heady, oppressive authority of a powerful creature. He was uncomfortable calling it a 'spirit' or a 'demon'; he didn't count himself a Christian, even if he had once been a church goer. He suspected that one day he'd return to the church, but if there was one group of people he felt really needed saving it was people with faith; he found he couldn't take them any more seriously than anyone who claimed to have the only truth.

If they really had the truth, then they were like children playing with a nuclear bomb – they knew what it did, but its *nature* was utterly beyond their understanding. So far beyond them they didn't even understand the depth of their ignorance.

Having said that, he knew his own ability to See was something he had been *given*, not born with, and the creatures he dealt with were more often than not anathema to humanity. If only he could have separated Christianity from its followers, then he might have been able to accept it.

Whatever was tied into the fabric of the place was immense. The dust shimmered with a blue-black authority, bound and angry. And Stephen was sure another entity was nearby, a teasing evanescence he couldn't pin down.

"There's more than one," he said to Harry.

"Aye," said the boy. "The big one was stuck here by the Christians."

Stephen could imagine their sense of achievement at binding the creature here. He could also picture their surprise when they were confronted with another demon upon their return to the farm house. He had a growing suspicion the second creature had gotten lucky; whoever had exercised authority against the being bound into the chapel was, for want of a better word, holy.

"I need to go outside," said Stephen.

"Why?" asked Harry, sharply.

"Got to check on what's keeping our beastie here," said Stephen.

He stepped out into the cold and started to walk around the building. He centred his mind and – as close to praying as he could bring himself – dwelt on the sensitivities he had been given when he had actively practised a faith. The sense of cleanliness washed over him; the rain was suddenly refreshing in its chill. Stephen slowed his pace around the chapel, letting his eyes focus. At each corner of the building were angels. He had once argued that they were nothing more than authorities who felt differently about humanity than the creature now bound into the church; these days he felt differently, that they were somehow an expression of that greater Authority and not wholly individuals in their own right. What he did know was that wherever they were, the greatest of authorities was present, and that they were a symbol of that regardless of their true natures.

He could hear, at the edge of his consciousness, the still, small voice whispering; it had always spoken, but he had decided long ago that its words were not for him. At times like these, he was tempted to give in and turn back, to listen, and to find out what had been hidden from the beginning. But temptation was not the same as paying the price.

He was glad to get back in the dry.

"Best tell your father not to dig or mess around in here, Harry," said Stephen. Harry was sat on the baptismal font, legs dangling carelessly. "Easiest thing is to leave out a saucer of unpasteurised milk each night. Your boggart'll be happy, then."

"You en't going to get rid of the other?" asked Harry. "It *wants* to be free. Says it wants to be in the city. Was a mistake coming here."

Stephen stood very still and looked at the boy. Watched him. "I'm sure it was," he said slowly. "But it would be better for everyone if it stayed right here. There's a story of a man who sent a host of monsters like this one into a herd of pigs. Never really understood it myself, the pigs stampeded down into a lake and died. What became of the monsters isn't made clear in the story. What the story does say, though, is that when those monsters are forced out but nothing takes their place, then they'll come back later with their bigger, badder, friends and really make themselves at home."

The boy shrugged. "It says it wants to go back to running corporations."

Stephen doubted the boy even knew what the word meant. "It is lying. Don't treat me like I'm a fool."

Harry jumped down from the font and advanced on Stephen, who suddenly felt a real sense of threat. "I'm trying to bargain with you," said the boy. "You can set me free or the boy will do it. The choice is yours, the outcome simple to understand."

"There are always other choices," said Stephen, backing away slowly in the direction of the door.

Harry laughed; a kitchen knife appeared in his hands.

"I've had enough of this," said Stephen firmly, as he reached the door. He pulled on the handle, but nothing moved. The mechanism turned easily enough, but the door was stuck fast.

"Have you made your choice?" asked Harry from a few feet behind him. "*You* could walk away from here, rather than this child. You have potential, we could influence people. Haven't you ever wanted that, to be influential?"

"Screw you," said Stephen, pulling again on

the door. He had a flash of Sight and dived away from the door as Harry thrust the knife at him. The blade sliced through thin air. Stephen jumped onto one of the pews and, using his elbow, punched at the window. The glaze crazed over, but the lead-work held it in place.

"I will *not* be bound here on a farm," said Harry angrily.

Stephen laughed. "It's that, isn't it? The indignity of being trapped in the middle of rural England" He looked around for some sort of weapon of his own; unfortunately, there was nothing that weighed less than a couple of hundred pounds at his disposal.

He tried one of the long pews and found he could just about lift it.

"Give it up," said Harry. "You're all alone out here, and no one is going to help you. No one even knows who you are."

Stephen grunted with the effort of dragging the pew. He got one arm underneath it, pulled it up high and stumbled as quickly as he could towards the window he'd already crazed. The pew struck the glass, and with an awful crunch, the lead-work burst out of its setting. Stephen dropped the bench and jumped at the window.

Harry screamed with a voice any self-respecting blues singer would have been proud of and rushed at Stephen's struggling body.

A curling ribbon of pain opened up on his leg as he fell out of the chapel into the mud outside the church. He could feel a shock of disconnection in his calf; it would be bleeding horrendously in moments, but Stephen didn't have moments.

Getting to his feet he ran, ignoring the pain, screaming when he couldn't, down the lane back towards the farm. He would warn the parents to keep people away from the chapel by phone. He'd also let them know that they could stop the boggart with a little milk left outside each night. Let the little bugger fight for it with local hedgehogs.

The blood had soaked through his trouser leg by the time he pulled out of the drive and back onto a real road half an hour later. He knew he ran the risk of doing himself permanent damage, but he wasn't going to stop until he reached civilisation.

Stewart Hotston

THE THREE QUEENS

Gill, his secretary – one of those older, single ladies who terrorise priests with invites for lunch on a Sunday morning after mass – had emailed him the file while he was driving south after an excursion to the countryside he would rather have forgotten.

The little car he was driving, a pale blue, three-door city runabout, was still complaining after the hammering he'd given it in his panic to be away from the remote farmhouse in Cumbria. A common-place boggart had been hiding a much more sinister beast he'd been lucky to get away from. Even then, three hours later, his hands were shaking after the run down the hill from the ruined chapel, where a small child had tried to rip his arms from his sockets.

He considered calling social services to have the child removed from the farm, but asked himself what the point would be.

I ought to have done my homework, he thought. *That thing nearly killed me.*

Someone had got there before him. He'd arrived in the aftermath of their bungling, which had in turn saved his life from a child who'd been intent on gutting him.

The car's tenuous hold on life slipped a little with every tortured gear change. He was half way down the M6 hogging the middle lane when Gill rang.

He wasn't a fan of breaking the law – he believed laws existed for a reason, generally to stop people doing stupid things they hadn't thought through. But like many people who considered themselves trustworthy, he thought nothing about answering the phone while doing eighty-five in a car which offered about as much protection as a damp cardboard box.

"Hi Gill."

"Hi. How did it go at the farm?"

"You were right, something funny was going

on." He didn't mention what he'd seen, and Gill didn't ask. To his eternal gratitude, she never did. She believed in the supernatural, but didn't want to be bothered with it. She was far more interested in the latest social horror unfolding on her television set in the east end of London.

"How much should I make your invoice out for?" He pictured her poised at the keyboard, and felt bad for disappointing her.

"Nothing. I didn't fix it for them. The problem was as much with them as the place." He thought again about social services and decided that even they didn't deserve what they'd find if they visited.

"I see. How much can we set aside for losses, then?"

"About five hundred. Time, petrol and general wear and tear."

There was silence on the other end of the phone. "We can afford to be generous..." he started.

"...You don't find it hard to make a decent living. There are literally billions of people out there who believe in something beyond the material world," finished Gill for him.

He sighed. "The ones that I help make up for the others." Most of the people who contacted him weren't really religious in the traditional sense, not in Britain, anyway. On infrequent jaunts overseas, often to Pakistan and India, he'd found other peoples were substantially more aware of what was going on around them, much more ready to assign it some place in their beliefs than dismiss it as mental illness.

England was, to his mind, still a bastion of the Church of England, even if most people didn't think of themselves that way anymore. But only a deluded fool would call the place a Christian nation. When asked, he'd describe it as a kind of gentle spirituality which prefers antiques and choirs at Christmas, fundraisers and moderation in all things. He'd quote a bishop he'd once met: "A true miracle is horrific – for all that it implies and all that it demands."

He would see those books and articles by vociferous materialists in the press, but thought them more humorous than enlightening. Regardless of people's feelings about spirituality, and even that peculiarly masculine trend for angrily insisting there's nothing more than atoms in this universe, he was overwhelmed by the number of calls his office received from week to week.

He'd written a spreadsheet in one of his quiet spells and figured he could take every job, invest the cash in tax-free accounts and live off the returns quite comfortably. To his own disgust, several of his peers had taken exactly that approach; and no one would question them, because they traded in the type of event that the devout take very seriously and are already prepared to deal with. He ended up handling everything else, dealing with those people who didn't want their local priest in, who didn't want prayers said and who didn't want to admit to anyone, let alone themselves, that they might actually be nothing more a temporary blotch of humanity in a vast world of other sentient creatures.

"I've got another one for you, so don't bother coming home."

"Where is it?"

"Wales. Rhyl. The Three Queens caravan park."

"Who the hell wants to go to Rhyl?" Silence on the other end. "That was a joke."

"The owner there, a Ms. Sudice, has asked for your help. They have a problem with housekeeping."

"Who would have thought it?" he said, thinking of baths and takeaways now to be missed. "And why do you think this one's worth my time?"

If he wished, he could be busy six days a

week just with the people who made it up in their heads, who needed to find someone to talk to or who just wanted some attention. He wouldn't even need to speak to those who'd be better off getting their lithium levels checked.

Most of what people thought was unnatural was neither unnatural nor especially mysterious. Rattling radiators that just needed bleeding, children moving things around to mess with people's heads. Even just a blind drunk not remembering things straight.

After seven years working for him, Gill had developed a fine sense for the mundane. She filtered all calls to the office via an artfully crafted checklist; twelve questions, which Gill claimed sorted the wheat from the chaff. The questions looked benign to him, but she was almost always right, so he left her to it and she let him get on with investigating.

There was little certainty he would be able to help; some of the things he encountered had an authority that only true believers could deal with and, in his experience, they were a rare breed: most of the faithful were just too concerned with gay sex or women having authority over men. It was that kind of nonsense that had seen his own exit from the church.

When asked, he'd avoid a straight answer.

He knew he had believed once, but it had been mucked up for him, mixed up with feelings of triumphalism and hand clapping. In the end he couldn't reconcile it with what he honestly thought faith was all about and, in feeling this, he found himself alone.

He suspected that one day he'd find himself sneaking back into a service somewhere, after the start, and trying to set everything straight with Himself. Even praying alone came with too many demands he wasn't in a place to respond to. Regardless, he found it hard to face spiritual entities who would eat his face off without harbouring the suspicion that one day he'd re-enter the folds of the good shepherd's cloak, but for the time being he was out on his own, carving his way through life, trying not to look too hard behind, nor too far ahead.

#

"So what's the problem?" he asked.

"*She claims that someone is wrecking their caravans.*"

"Gill," he started, impatiently. "This doesn't sound promising."

"*Hold your horses,*" she said, sternly. "*The caravans are being wrecked on the* inside, *on nights when they're unoccupied. It's not local kids, and it's not staff. At least, not as far as they can tell. The trailers remain locked throughout, and there are only three master keys on site. Look, they can tell you themselves, but I think there's enough here to warrant your time."*

He subsided, still not convinced, but he was closer to the caravan park than home. The thought of getting home only to have another day of driving did not appeal.

"I quoted a grand a day and said it would be two days minimum. They agreed."

"No haggling?"

"None," she said, a little smugly.

Cash was the only real test he believed in. Gill frequently took calls from time-wasters and skeptics, but found – after her checklist – that the list of charges made most stories of ghosts bumping about in the night suddenly less compelling. Half of all calls hung up at that point. Another forty percent started to argue about the price, and Gill would make a judgement call; she couldn't stand the thought of someone truly being harassed and not being able to afford the help they needed. The last ten percent simply accepted the costs.

He felt for the last group. He asked himself

just how bad would things have to be for someone to be charged a grand a day to deal with something they didn't even *believe* in and conclude 'that's fine.'

When he'd started out, he thought it an outrageous price, but there were so many callers willing to pay, he eventually stopped thinking about it. Besides, it was how he kept Gill and Sophie, his researcher, employed. Gill took five thousand calls a year. Of those, she quoted for just ten percent, and of those, about fifty took it on the chin like champions. They went straight to the top of the list. Some were busts, like the one he was escaping from in Cumbria, but either way, the average job lasted two to five days. Fifty times a year.

"Ok, I'm listening."

"Nothing more than that, really. No deaths, no injuries, no slime, ooze or faeces. Messed up furniture, water left to overflow and opened windows."

Someone could just be getting in through the windows, he thought.

"Windows open from the inside, and the locks are still locked but have somehow been detached from the frame," said Gill, carrying on. *"Sophie's still trying to work it out. She's dialling in now."*

He could hear Sophie talking in the background. A girl-next-door type, of the kind that men found irresistible. She was, as far as he could tell, utterly disinterested in sex and love except as she devoured it through medieval romances.

"Hiya. Bad day?" She was Dutch, and sounded like she'd never had a bad day in her life.

"Kind of. What've you got for me?"

"Not sure. Obviously Sudice is a name I recognise."

"Obviously." He didn't, but something about Sophie always made him want to appear smarter than he really was.

"Good. Good. I don't understand the upheaval they're facing, though. Look for something threatening the status quo."

There wasn't much more to say except to get directions for the satnav, so he hung up and continued driving.

#

The caravan park wasn't anywhere near Rhyl, as it turned out. He drove past Anglesey and kept going until he thought the satnav was going drive him into the sea, eventually reaching the end of a desolate headland. He pulled up on the edge of a hamlet, wondering if it was Ireland he could see on the horizon.

He'd arrived at Abersoch. *Sounds German*, he thought.

Abersoch was a one-horse town where the horse had died. The caravan park was half a mile down the road, inland and perched on a hill overlooking the town. The roads were narrow and high-sided, except for along the coast where they fell precipitously into the sea. It was getting dark as he pulled up. He had tried to stop for dinner on the way, but it was deepest, darkest Wales in the low season with not a scrap to be found. He wasn't fussy, fish and chips would have been more than welcome, but as he rolled into Abersoch at around ten in the evening, he was grumpy, tired and very, very hungry.

He thought fondly of his neighbourhood in London. Twenty-four hour delis, takeaways and people who were already drunk before he got up in the morning. He routinely experienced a shiver whenever he crossed the M25, like traversing the border to a foreign land where the people were all in bed by midnight, only needed to shop during the day, and weren't ever desperate for lemon-stuffed olives at one in the morning.

The street that ran past the caravan park wasn't lit. A garish, perfectly awful neon sign featuring painfully bad depictions of Freddie Mercury, Elton John and someone he didn't recognise but suspected was Liberace flashed in green, yellow and pink under a blue sign that welcomed him to the Three Queens. As he parked up between a VW Campervan and a Chelsea tractor, which didn't have a single spatter of mud, he contemplated the mind which considered that sign a worthwhile investment.

Without the engine turning over, the windows in the car started to mist up. Heaving the sigh of a day spent driving on Britain's regional roads, he got out and stretched his arms and legs.

It was a cool, sea-sprayed autumn evening far from artificial lighting, and the stars were twinkling in shameless glory like an audience suddenly revealed to the players in the theatre. The Irish Sea crashed against the headland, an inconsistent roar that he found more grating than the trucks which rumbled along his own road in the early morning.

A small shack stood at the edge of the car park; a bulb hanging by a single wire glowed the colour of stale pee. Beyond that, he could see lights from four caravans. He guessed, from the gaps in the darkness, that there were at least another eight of them. The large silhouette of a house blocked out stars further up the hill.

A door in the shack opened up to reveal a short, elderly man. "Can I help you?" he called out.

"Hi." He pulled his overnight bag from the back seat of the car and walked over. The old man played with a ring of keys while he waited, eventually going back into the shack a couple of steps ahead of his new guest.

"I'm Curaim, the caretaker." He sat, like a building site foreman, behind a rickety chipboard desk, which looked as if it had started life as a wallpaper bench. An ancient white electric kettle, a plain red mug and a newspaper were the only things on its surface. A jar of instant coffee perched on a small filing cabinet in the corner. The room smelt of burnt rubber. A grey plastic chair sat on the other side of the desk, undersized even for a child. Sitting, his knees higher than his shoulders, he looked at the caretaker expectantly.

"Hi, I'm here about the caravans. I was told to ask for Mrs Sudice?"

The caretaker nodded. "She wondered if you'd come tonight. We have a caravan for you, free of charge, of course." Curaim looked at him, his expression asking what he'd done with his life to warrant the honour.

"Great." He didn't really have anything else to do. "Is there anywhere I can get some food?"

"It's very late." There was a teasing tone in his voice. "But we did save you some sandwiches. I'll have them brought down to number 5."

"Is that where I'm sleeping?"

"I hope so." He laughed.

"I assume it's the caravan where the events have been happening?"

He stopped laughing, suddenly serious. "You're really good."

#

They wandered down to the caravan, a long circuitous route that left him feeling disoriented until he caught sight of the sign on the road and the light from the office fifty metres away. He was too tired and hungry to ask why they'd walked the long way around.

#

Once inside, he found he could barely turn around without bumping into something. The caravan turned out to be one that would have been more comfortable on someone's drive in suburbia. He was bitterly unsurprised to see the word *Conqueror* written in Comic Sans on the side.

He stood in the middle of the floor, unable

to decide whether to leave his bag by his feet so he'd have to step over it every time he went from the bathroom to the bed, or to leave it on the table so that he'd have to eat off his lap. There was a knock at the door.

A white plate was thrust at him. He took it gratefully, and looked up to find that whoever had delivered it was already a retreating shadow in the night. Shutting the door, he looked at the offering: white bread turning up at the corners, sliced into triangles, with a thin grey spread gluing them together. The bread was on the turn, but he was too hungry to care and ate them in one go.

The mattress was bouncy and soft, which was just how he hated them. The curtains, where they covered the window, were thin. The fitful neon of the sign streamed. He slept fitfully and woke with the dawn.

#

It was raining the next morning. Grey beads of water that blew, in billows of salty mist, straight off the sea to soak the skin of those huddled under umbrellas. He numbly pulled on his clothes, trying – in vain, as it turned out – to find clean underwear. He stumbled out into the morning in search of breakfast, wishing he'd brought his good coat instead of his thin hoody.

He fell into line with a family of six: mum, dad and four kids ranging from a babe in arms to a girl just hitting puberty. Their accents suggested the northwest of England. Seeing them head for the house, he tagged along behind them, keeping his head down and huddling within his coat as best as he could. The father was hairy, like a Wookiee, and he entertained himself wondering if the bulge in the back of his jeans was a tail.

The house was smaller than it appeared from the outside, built of brick and covered in dirty white pebbledash up to the first floor. The pitch roof was old red tiles, and dormer windows peeked out from either side of a capped chimney stack. He found himself in a large dining room converted out of a PVC conservatory bolted on to the back of the house. His stomach gurgled at the smell of bacon.

A small woman, looking even older than the ancient caretaker, grabbed hold of his arm with crooked fingers. "Did you bring plate with you?"

"I'm sorry, it's still in the caravan." He felt for the phone in his pocket, having a sudden urge to check for messages.

"You sleep okay, then?"

"I did." He assumed she was Mrs Sudice. She seemed surprised at his answer.

"Breakfast comes out of your fee?"

"Sundries are additional, Mrs. Sudice." Her grip didn't lessen. Holding onto him like a hawk clutchin an unlucky rabbit, she steered them out of the dining room and into the kitchen. Two more women were there; one was around his age, which was older than he was happy with but still younger than he thought of as 'old.' The second woman was just about twenty. They were three generations of the same family, sharing the same bent noses, high cheeks and thin, unhappy lips.

"Morning, love," said the middle-aged one, also short, but not as shrunken by age as her mother. She had brown hair tied up in a bun and, underneath her apron, wore a thick brown woollen jumper and light grey sweat pants. 'You want everything, do you?" Her accent sounded about as Welsh as his did.

"Please."

The old woman shoved him at the table and pushed him firmly into one of the wooden chairs surrounding the room's battered, stained centrepiece. When he was seated, her claws let go. He imagined an audible pop. She whisked off out of the room to see to her paying customers.

"Don't mind Ma. This whole thing's got her agitated. Sunny side up?"

"Cooked through, please, crispy if possible." He hated runny yolks and slimy eggs.

"I'm Liz, and my young 'un is Mary." Mary smiled at him while reaching up into a cupboard to grab a party-size box of tea bags. "You should probably call Ma 'Mrs Sudice.' If she likes you, she'll let you call her Ma."

"Her first name is Anne," said Mary, pulling half a dozen bags from the box and dumping them into a large metal teapot already full of hot water. "None of us get to call her that, though."

"Don't be bothering him with that," said Liz. He was having a hard time concentrating, as she was plating up breakfast while she spoke. The sight of sausages, bacon, black pudding, eggs and fried bread made him dizzy, and there wasn't a tomato in sight.

I might actually enjoy this trip, he thought.

With a clink, the plate landed in front of him.

He abandoned any pretence of professionalism in favour of wolfing down the food; normally he would have asked the women to talk about the problem. Fortunately, he discovered as he shoved in half a sausage, they didn't need encouragement.

"It started about a month ago," said Mary,

getting a look from her mother that he took to mean she should have waited to be asked. Ignoring the expression as only children can, she continued. "At the end of the summer, when the first of the caravans turned vacant. We tidied it as we always do and locked up for the winter. We weren't expecting anyone else in that unit until next year. The next morning, Bill comes hobbling in, saying the bricks under the wheels had been messed with. Mum wandered down to take a look and, on the off chance, she peered through one of the windows."

"Carnage," said Liz, taking up the story.

"The table was torn from the floor," said Mary.

"They're nailed down," added Liz. "The curtains had been pulled from their rails and the sink blocked up; the water'd run until it was overflowing. The water shouldn't have even been connected. Bill swears he disconnected it."

"We couldn't get in, either, because the key was in the shack. Bill ran back to get it, but that was when it struck us as odd. How had someone got in to do all that when the door was still locked?"

Mary laughed. "We did, for a moment, imagine Bill letting himself in for a bit of rock and roll." The thought of the old guy tearing the place up was hard to hold onto. "He was so upset."

"We all were. We tidied up, but the water damage meant there wasn't a lot we could do." Liz served herself and Mary a plate of bacon and eggs. They sat down around the table and tucked in.

Between mouthfuls, Liz continued the story. "Damage like that means an insurance claim and a new caravan. It's not an easy thing to get the smell of damp chipboard out of such a small space."

He finished up with a wipe down of the plate with a slice of buttered bread. In the moment of contentment that followed, he reverted to his normal process. It was fine that the two women were corroborating each other's story, but all that really meant was they'd talked about it, ironed out any points on which they disagreed.

He preferred to take the temperature of the witnesses, get a feel for their impressions and then go see for himself. His gift was personal, he had no need for divining rods or tarot cards. He held such things in disdain; they were little more than guff other people thought was a hotline to whatever it was they believed in. Quite what powers they thought would concern themselves with badly-drawn middle-class erotica plastered on a piece of cardboard was beyond him. He'd never encountered mystical energies, benign or otherwise, and was a big fan of going to a doctor who relied on evidence-based medicine.

"I can see that you're busy," he said. "Do you mind if I look around?"

Liz nodded. Mary began to clear away their plates. Although it was the twilight of the holiday season, they were about half-booked for the week, and it was obvious that they had a lot to do.

He let himself out through the kitchen, discovering a small, fenced-off garden half paved over with pebbledash concrete. A gate at the far end of the garden let him back into the park proper. He was confronted with a large building site: mud, sand and blocks of bricks piled up on one another across an area that was easily as big as the entire caravan park. A digger sat unused on the other side of a low wire fence.

He turned away from the abandoned building site and made his way along the wooden fence to the grass covering most of the caravan park. He was surprised to see that, apart from the one he'd been in, most of the caravans were pretty sizeable. Most were fixed homes that couldn't be moved without a powerful engine. They'd been delivered to the Three Queens to spend the rest of their lives.

Pulling his phone out he dialled Sophie, to see if she could put the symptoms into context. Powers didn't act up, in the main, without reason. It might not be a reason ordinary people would understand or care about, but powers had their own way of seeing the world.

He grunted with annoyance at the lack of signal. A flash of very weak wi-fi, but it was password protected. He was cut off.

He rambled up the steep hillside to the highest point on site, so he could see the whole park in one go. Catching his breath against the wind and the exertion, he closed his eyes and concentrated; allowing his gift to come to the fore.

The gift, as he thought of it, was the capacity to see things as they truly were. It wasn't something he used often, for fear of his own sanity. He tried not to use it at all, if he could help it, and avoided getting involved in cases in heavily built-up areas. In his mind it was a gift from God, although he didn't count himself as Godly.

Opening his eyes, he gazed down on the park and gasped. The caravan park was full of those powers who simmered somewhere between active hatred of mankind and working towards humanity's good. Hovering over the house were half a dozen telltale signs of non-human authority; faint puffs of colour painted over the real world like fingerprints on a canvas. The three women were at the heart of it, but they weren't the only ones. The rest of the park was dotted with similar individuals. To his amazement, he realised he was the only mortal in the Three Queens. The Wookiee from breakfast was suddenly a much less ridiculous character. This far from civilisation, he'd expected to find nothing more than those wisps of creation that were so ephemeral it would be hard to say they were truly creatures at all.

He hurried down the hillside, muddying his trousers and, despite the persistent cold rain blowing into his face, working up a sweat. He slowed as he got to the house, his impulse to confront the women draining away as his brain caught up with his emotions.

He stood at the back door, hand on the door handle, unable to walk inside. He looked at the wall, trying to imagine who and what they actually were. The door opened, pulling away from his hand.

Mary stood in the doorway. "Are you going to come in?" she asked.

He suddenly realised that Mary was beautiful in a way her mother was not. Her mother, Liz, had the kind of smooth skin that most women her age would die for, but her features were slightly too small. She struck him as having too much face.

Mary, in contrast, had large hazel eyes and long natural lashes, her cheek bones were high without being angular and her lips reminded him of Cupid's bow. Hair styled as though it were nineteen fifty shone even in the dim light of the rainy morning. Her body was hidden beneath a long, loose-fitting t-shirt, but he could make out its curves and his chest tightened as he ran his eyes over her. He was old enough to be her father, but couldn't stop imagining their bodies entwined.

Shaking his head, he said, "Stop it, Mary."

She frowned, and in that moment he remembered she was not merely an object to judge against her mother; but nor was she human. "Who are you?" she asked, fear crawling the edges of her face. He was highly recommended in certain circles, but he was careful to keep the scope of his gift hidden.

"I'm the guy you rang."

She stepped back, let him in to the kitchen.

Liz was there, as was Ma. They didn't speak as he sat himself down at the table, being sure to keep all three of them in his field of view as he did so. "Why don't you start by telling me who you *are*."

The women looked at one another for some moments before Ma started muttering angrily at the other two in a language that sounded like Russian but wasn't. He suddenly wished he'd asked Sophie why she'd recognised the family name.

Liz started to reply to her mother in their

shared language. "Speak English," said Mary in an exasperated tone. "*You* rang him."

The other two glared at her, the air taking on a turgid hostility. It had happened before; people would ring him but not be sure they wanted him there, even *after* he'd finished his work for them. The hair on the back of his neck crawled, demanding he run as fast as he could. Instead he grasped the table with his hands until the knuckles went white.

Mary was having none of it. "Don't give me that, either. He comes here, works out our big secret in half an hour and now you want to hide from him? Are you serious?"

The tension in the air wilted away and he started breathing again. Liz and Ma pursed their lips, mother and daughter reflecting each other perfectly.

"Why don't you tell them what you've figured out," said Mary, turning to him. "It might help them relax." He didn't agree, but sometimes the customer's right even when they're wrong.

"You're family. Three women, none of whom have men in their lives." He found it hard to say difficult truths straight out to people's faces, so tended to start with easier ones and work his way up. "You've been here several decades and although people *do* leave, and even come back occasionally, your guests don't notice that you haven't aged since you arrived. Mary, I doubt you've changed your hairstyle for as long as I've been alive." Ma glared at him. "I've no care that you're not human, and I'm not here to take sides or send you away. I'm actually pro immigration. I came because you called me, and my assistant believed your story. Evidence of which I've seen no sign of, by the way."

"It happened," said Liz.

"I'm sure *something* happened, but I'm left wondering why you'd ring me when the three of you, together, have told authorities capable of ripping the world apart where to get off."

"See?" said Mary throwing her hands in the air. To him, she said, "Our authority is narrow, little one, limited to reflections of our purpose."

Liz sat down at the table with him, as did Mary. Ma waited, statue-still, eyes following him around the room. "Ma, come and sit."

"I mean you no harm."

Mary laughed at him, half in disbelief and half without trust. "Understand, I could call Christians and ask them to come visit." The temperature in the room dropped a couple of degrees.

"Few of them talk to Him like that," said Ma

calmly.

"'Few' is not 'none,' though is it, Ma? I could bring them here and you know what they'd do with you. They'd see it as a kindness." The eyes of the three women glittered, waiting. "Perhaps it would be. This world is not one for you right now, and He works beyond my understanding anyway. But I won't call them unless you lie to me again." It was a bluff; apart from anything else, his phone had no signal. He couldn't even say what they'd do; the woman he was thinking of was a prophet, although she hated being called that. She'd know what was happening within five minutes of arriving and then she'd do something that would terrify anyone with an ounce of sense: the woman of God would ask God what to do, and He would answer her.

"Fine." Ma's accent was from far to the east of Wales. Within it, he could hear floating mountains, misty rivers and forgotten wars. Suddenly the room smelled of snow and death, of forgotten bones sticking out of the ground in marshes fought over long ago. "If you betray us, I shall tell you the manner of your death."

Mary rolled her eyes. Her grand-daughter could afford to be blasé, but he had no wish to know the future, so he nodded and waited for them to tell their story.

Liz began. "We came here from Croatia some

years ago. The Schengen Accord was good for us. Your country has more people in it than we'd thought, always so busy. Always bustling and rushing about somewhere. So many new memories that old ones get pushed out, lost and discarded." She sounded horrified. "Yet your passion for the new makes room for us."

"So you bought the land and some caravans?"

"No." Ma shook her head. "The caravans already here. We changed name and cleaned up mess of those who sold it. Very disgusting people before us." She made a sign with her hand that perfectly conveyed just how revolting they were.

"Why here?" he asked.

"Is quiet!" said Ma triumphantly.

"She means," said Liz. "That in a nation of information and immanence, prone to forgetting what happened yesterday, this town – this caravan park – is especially forgotten. We're happy here, with no one pestering us, none seeking their fortunes from us. We're sparks floating alone far from the bonfire that gave us life; one day that fire shall return and claim us, but until then, in the world as you've remade it, we're happy to sit quietly."

"He knows what I mean."

"I do." He was touched. He was certain there was more to their story, but it was enough to understand the life they were leading there and then. "Have you spoken with the creature wrecking your park?"

"We have. We"re not in a position to order it about."

"You invited it here."

"We invited them all here." Mary sounded less than impressed. "Fortunately only a few took us up on our offer, but as it is, half the caravans are occupied throughout the year. I'm not even sure what some of them are, and I can remember the fall of Rome."

"You're still only a youth," said Liz.

"Has the impatience only the young feel," said Ma, agreeing.

"I'm just not convinced we should risk drawing attention to ourselves," said Mary.

"People don't want to know about you," he said, certain that the last thing Generation Television wanted was for their fantasy shows to be true.

"It's not *people* I'm worried about," said Liz.

"Which caravan does it stay in?"

The women looked at one another. "We thought it would come to you last night but you are tidy man."

"Ah." They'd given him the crappiest caravan in the park, because it was the one the creature kept wrecking. "I keep a tidy house." He stood up, full of the need to act. "That's easily rectified – give me a tin of beans and it'll be in the caravan before I've closed my eyes for the night. Can you tell me if I can get a phone signal in the village?"

Mary laughed. "We've got wi-fi. I'll give you the password." He took the password, excused himself, and left the Three Queens through the front gate. He walked down the hill towards town, passing the building site on his right. He was impressed by just how considerate the builders were; they had left bricks in piles, there wasn't a trace of rubbish and even the diggers, mixers and skips were lined up. A hoarding next to the road announced they were building thirty-six new two- and three-bedroom homes. He was from London and used to buildings springing up from one week to the next; here, on the verge of a small road in quietest Wales, three dozen new houses were a big deal.

He carried on past the site, wondering just how out of place such a development was. His skin itched at the thought of those houses standing empty. The glassless windows and empty doorways carried an air of desolation that only actual people living in them, making them homes, could press down and overcome. Houses that had never been lived in not only lacked souls, they leered at his own frailty, calling out that their loss could be his as well.

In the village, he was delighted to find a post office and corner shop, together with a tiny little pub stuffed into someone's front room. The place was empty, dimly lit, with a smell of long-banned cigarette smoke, like cherished but mostly forgotten anecdotes. The pint the barmaid pulled for him looked like any anywhere.

"Hi Sophie, it's me."

"Hi, you." She sounded happy, as usual. He explained about the entity driven to wreck the caravans.

"With a name like Sudice, I think you're looking at a kikimora. It's a household spirit that rewards women who keep a tidy house and plagues those who don't." She sounded like she was holding the receiver under her chin while flicking through websites. *"You need to tell them to stop leaving everything in such a mess."*

"They're way beyond that. They know what she is and how to handle it. This one's playing up, wrecking the place when there's no reason. They're interested in calming it down."

Sophie was typing in the background.

"You need to figure out what's disturbing it. If it's not a physical mess, maybe she's disturbed by something else." The barmaid gave him a look that suggested only people from big cities came into her pub and spent their time talking on their phones.

A thought was starting to form, so heeding the glare he hung up and drank the rest of his bitter in silence.

#

He took dinner in his 'palace.' He didn't mind the three women, from a professional point of view, but he wasn't a social person. He found it hard enough to be around people he *liked*, let alone creatures whose origin Darwin had never imagined. On his better days, he could manage small groups, but they were liable to leave him tongue-tied and frustrated.

When he was done with the stew they'd delivered to the caravan, he cracked open the tins of lager from the off-licence. The night came on; around ten, he decided the time was about right and proceeded to throw his rubbish on the floor, being careful to empty his travel bag on the tiny sofa and leave his receipt on the table with that day's crumpled newspaper.

He tucked himself up in his bed and waited. As he was drifting off, he caught the smell of nutmeg, and then nothing.

He awoke to the sound of cracking glass. Sitting bolt upright, he smacked his head on the top bunk bed with a crack that knocked him flat. He lay there for a moment, feeling for blood and trying to stop himself from shouting out in pain.

With a groan, he rolled out of the bed and onto his knees. "You can stop, I'll tidy up. I only wanted to talk." A soft moaning suffused the air. He could smell fresh bread and the sharp citrus of hopeful mornings. "Thanks." He got to his feet. There was no sign of his visitor. "You can show yourself, I've got privileges."

He'd found that few authorities responded to his honest opening gambit, and the kikimora wasn't any different, so he closed his eyes and let his sight shift into the realm of the true. He opened them to see a short, hunched woman stood in front of him, her face more hornbill than human, with a large, thin beak curving down towards the floor. Her eyes were hidden by the hood of her storm cloak. Stick-like fingers protruded from the cloak's sleeves, brown and shrivelled to the bone.

"This is your home. Why are you wrecking it?" She was between him and the seats; he thought about perching on the bottom bunk, but it was too low down to confidently challenge a creature like this. So, head thumping, he remained standing.

She chattered like a starling, high and shrill; rapid, staccato tweets that he couldn't make sense of. The tone was clear though – she was unhappy.

"I know you're unhappy, we all do." He smiled in the gloom. "The Sudice have given you a home. I promised them I'd talk to you and find out what's wrong. You can't mess with their home, it's all any of you have got."

She swayed from side to side like an animal in a cramped cage at a zoo. Frustration and despair ate at the air.

"Can you show me?" he asked. She may have no access to words. With one last swoon, she moved through the wall of the caravan. He followed, using the door, and found her sweeping across the park towards the boundary. He ran to keep up.

She reached the edge of the park and stopped, with a keening cry that tingled in the fingers. There wasn't anything to see, just the chain link fence and the building site beyond it. The kikimora floated by the fence and looked out onto the churned earth on the other side.

On a hunch, he clumsily climbed over the fence and found one of the neat piles of bricks he'd been impressed by earlier. Eyes fixed on the kikimora, he tipped one off the top of a cube of stacked bricks. He was ready to step back, but she moved faster than he'd anticipated. The kikimora changed colour, glowing the deep red of a hot coal bed and charged at him, a raging scream filling the air as she came. He ducked away, covering his head as she passed over him and started to rip the building site apart. He watched, through his fingers, as she up turned the bricks, flinging them around like pebbles. The racket of masonry smashing into mud like raindrops in a spring storm convinced him to get the hell out of there. He sprang to his feet, flinched as a black shape came winging towards him and heard, more than felt, a crunch just above his right eye.

#

"He's alright." A gruff welsh voice.

"Christ, look at that gash on his head." Another Welshman's voice, with less added gravel.

"Make sure he's okay."

He opened his eyes, rainwater spilling down his face. A beard, was his first impression. Hard hats followed, with high visibility jackets. His head felt numb.

"You alright, there?"

"I think so," he croaked.

"That was some tornado that came through here last night." The eyes watched for a reaction. He wasn't up to reacting – his body was busy telling him, via the medium of pain, that hunches were not to be followed from that point onwards. "What were you doing here, anyway? The site was closed."

"Just interested in seeing what you were building," he managed.

"Can you stand?" He nodded and allowed himself to be pulled to his feet. He wanted to feel his forehead, but knew that if he found blood he might lose his composure, and then his footing. He'd been there before, and knew that as long as he didn't really *know* he was injured, he'd likely be able to carry on regardless. It was when the mind figured it out, properly realised, that he'd find himself bedridden.

"Where're you from?" He could see other people on site now. Two of them, clearly baffled were inspecting an overturned excavator, while others were half-heartedly picking up plaster board, cinder blocks and other debris. They weren't trying too hard, as it was difficult to make out the ground through the wreckage. The kikimora had partied like it was the end of the world.

"Queens," he half-said. The fellow nodded and, after wrapping his forehead in gauze, walked him back to the front door of the Sudice's house.

Bill saw them coming into the car park. He took a couple of steps in their direction before turning around, then around again, and once more. Then he rushed into the house ahead of them as fast as his legs would carry him.

#

A mug of builder's tea warmed chilled hands. The kitchen was hot and humid, for which he was truly thankful. His clothes, mud-stained and soaking, were in the washing machine, while he took refuge in a large duvet.

"Did you object to the development?" he asked the three Sudice.

They shared a look. "No," said Liz, "there wasn't any warning. We woke one morning to find them digging."

He sighed. "Do you remember seeing any little yellow sheets of plastic with writing on them stuck to lampposts?"

Mary frowned. "Maybe. Why?" The other two looked at him as if he was about to explain the Big Bang to them.

"You could have stopped it." It was too late by this point. His job had changed; it was now to find a way of telling them the bad news. Getting paid was starting to look like a long shot.

"Why would we want to do that?" asked Mary, genuine confusion on her face. Ma muttered something in Croatian.

"Your kikimora. What's her name?" He always asked, it was a thing with him. Somehow it made everything about the creatures who were beyond him in so many ways a little bit more manageable – to know that someone, somewhere, could call them by a name that truly belonged to them.

"Darija." Liz's eyes were red-rimmed.

He said her name, felt it roll on the tongue. "She can't live with you anymore. The building site is upsetting her."

Mary laughed, a sharp outburst. "You think? She was proper carnage there."

"It won't stop. She's been acting up because of the encroaching building work, but couldn't take her fear and frustration out on the builders, because they've been so tidy." He almost couldn't believe he was saying it. "She came in response to one of your invites?" They nodded. "Like you, she wanted somewhere lost, to be at peace."

"What can we do?" asked Mary.

He didn't have an answer – it was past time to try to stop the building. "I don't know." He spoke on before they could interrupt. "What I *do* know is that, unless those builders tidy the site up perfectly, she's not going to stop. They'll figure something's going on here eventually."

Ma sat down heavily. "We cannot send her away." She made no attempt to hide her accent.

"I'm sorry." They ignored him, and he sat and watched as they argued back and forth about whether they could send the forlorn house spirit away, but Ma was as hard as granite.

"I will not have her sent away. She is family."

"There are places in Scotland she could go," he ventured. The offer was met with silence.

"We do not look for the same things as you from our homes," said Mary, voice cold and hostile, shoving him away with a stiff reminder that he was the hired help, a mortal they'd called in and who had given them news that shattered their peace.

She was right; he would have known the building site butting onto their land would upset their delicately structured isolation. But these three didn't think about the world like humans. They still saw things in terms of rites, rituals and the rhythms of nature. It wouldn't have ever occurred to them that the building site was to blame, because they didn't really understand the concept. The kikimora had seen the homes being built and had felt the inevitability of being sucked back into the role it had played for centuries elsewhere. It had come to the Three Queens to escape that fate, only to find it arriving on the doorstep like an estranged family member.

He wanted to leave, but couldn't bring himself to, knowing it would appear like he was trying to escape from their misery.

"We came here to rest, away from your kind, to live quietly." The bitterness in Mary's voice was palpable.

After another fifteen minutes of awkward silence, he pushed his chair back. "I'm going to go pack. I'll come back when I'm ready to go." They didn't look up as he left, still wrapped in his duvet.

\#

They had moved to the guest dining room by the time he returned. "What have you decided?" he asked.

Ma didn't turn to acknowledge him and Mary folded her arms, her lips pursed. Liz spoke. "We're going to move. All of us; we invited them here, and we have a responsibility to give them the sanctuary they came for. We don't know where, but Ma is right. Now is not the time to abandon our own. We came here looking for a refuge in these cold, hard times." And even here, far from prying eyes, they were being pushed out. "You should go." Her words were hard, and bitter as lemon pith.

He nodded, half raised his hand to say goodbye before stopping himself; they didn't care.

As he packed the car, he occasionally paused to gaze at the house, not sure what he was looking for except to obey the insistent tug that there was something he should see.

Whatever time I spend with these creatures, he thought, *beings who spend their lives on the margins of creation, shoved there by our blind insistence that they don't exist, they remain impossible for me to connect to.* Sadness lay over the caravan park, thicker than the miserable clouds overhead.

He wondered if refugees remain alien to their hosts because that way they don't have to connect with them, to make it safer to turn away.

He was scared about what the answer said of him.

The air stirred, and he knew the kikimora was nearby. He spoke to the emptiness in front of him, hoping he was facing the right way. "You should go with them. They'll look after you." He didn't want to use his gift to see her again, so tried to speak so she wouldn't have to respond. "I'm sorry about this. We're everywhere, forgetting what we knew, forgetting how to make your life easier." The air stirred and settled. While he had been speaking, Liz had come out from the house.

"Darija likes you." She pressed her lips together in a thin smile. "You're not what I anticipated."

He smiled, unsure where she was going. She folded her arms across her chest and rested her weight on one leg. "I think she will be calm, now she knows we're leaving."

"I can help."

"We can't afford to pay you more than we've already agreed."

He shrugged, undecided about his offer, not sure if he meant it regardless of the money.

"You could come visit sometime." She smiled at him; an offer of friendship, of mutual respect. "When we've found somewhere new."

"I'd like that." He knew what it was to be on the outside looking in.

#

He rang them the next day, after a very hot, long bath and a good curry, on the number they'd used to contact Gill. He'd found half a dozen places he thought they might be able to settle and wanted to make sure they fit whatever requirements they had. Gill watched him with approval, but was wise enough not to openly comment.

Liz answered the phone and said, with just a hint of sisterly mischief, "I'll get Mary. She was wanting to talk to you."

FARM BOY

He chopped at the wood with a ferocious determination, his swing easy, intent, unrelenting. The woodpile shrank quickly until he was standing, sweaty and dazed, in the shadows of the barn.

He looked around for something else to work on, but saw nothing; the concentration slowly drained from his body. He snatched a rag hanging over a wooden rail to dry off.

Once the worst of his exertion had been mopped away, Elliot shuffled the top few wedges around, stacking them thin end in to improve the stability of the pile. He checked the axe was secure in the block and then stepped out of the barn into the hard sunshine of an unseasonably hot autumn day.

Jack wouldn't be back from town until sundown; knowing that didn't make the waiting any easier.

"What're you doing?" asked Marya's voice from the house. He turned to look at her, shielding his eyes from the sun. He didn't need to answer; she knew why he was so anxious. "He'll get the foretelling he's destined to get, Elliot. No point you fretting over it, won't change a thing."

He snorted heavily. "It's not like I don't know," he said. "I already lost one argument today. I'm not fixing to lose a second before lunch."

She shook her head. "Wasn't an argument you were ever going to win, Elliot Greengrass; I don't know why you tried."

"That's the point, ain't it. Got to try," said Elliot.

"How's that working for you?" she asked.

He didn't answer. Instead he gazed across the farm land, past the barn and newly finished stables, down the hill towards the workers' cottages at the woodland to the south, as if by sheer concentration he might make the trees vanish so to reveal the distant silhouette of Shatterborough five miles away.

"Don't just stand there, Elliot, chores won't

get done by themselves. You know this weather won't last forever. Rains are coming and the fences along Barin's land need setting upright." She dusted her hands as if she were done with him. "I'm going to see to my pies, when I come back you shouldn't be anywhere I can see you." With a finality that had him moving before she'd gone back into the house, she turned and closed the lower half of the door behind her.

#

He managed to lose himself down by the brook, hoisting dead wood from under the stone bridge that crossed over it. The stonework was undamaged, although from this angle he could see one of the dry stone walls needed some attention around its base.

Elliot muttered to himself over the water level; it had been a dry summer and his neighbours upstream had created a pond to breed trout. It seemed to him they had forgotten other people also relied on the water coming down the channel: not just him, but the next farm along too. They had a well for the farmhouse but the animals needed watering, as did what crops they grew – beet, a few potatoes and carrots. Kitchen vegetables. Their money was in the livestock.

At some point over the next week, he'd have to go over there and ask them to open up the sluice gates a touch. He didn't mind them farming their fish, and they'd always got on well enough, but it was a journey he could do without.

Elliot worked bare-backed, slowly lifting the fence posts back into place and stretching the wire between them taut. Scars across his back pulled as he strained against the tension but he was built strong and made quick work of it.

It was dusk before he was finished. He looked up, taking in the reddening sky with a sense of inevitability. He was happy at least that the afternoon hadn't dragged him along moment by moment.

The ragged edge to his satisfaction was how Jack would be home, news to tell. He managed to distract himself with the thought that he was more interested in the money Jack should have made from selling hens eggs and Marya's baking. He wondered how much salt he'd brought back with him, or if Ben Smith had been able to rummage up three dozen nails as he'd promised.

The evening had settled on the farm by the time he walked into the yard. An amiable yellow lamplight shone through the kitchen windows, giving the night a blue weight. The smell of stewing apples made Elliot's mouth water well before he opened the kitchen door and let himself in.

"Ah, the wanderer has returned," said Marya warmly.

Elliot looked around for Jack before realising she was talking about him.

"Where is he?"

"Upstairs. Found himself a book in town."

"Ha," laughed Elliot. "I can never remember if words are my enemy or my friend."

"Depends on whether you're arguing with me," said Marya without hesitation.

He nodded to himself, and at the sight of a linen wrapped block of salt by the door, asked "How'd he do?"

"Didn't talk about it," said Marya blandly, "but he got the nails. Ben threw in an invitation to get the horses shod before winter as well."

"He's a good one," said Elliot, although it didn't need saying.

"You've done your part," said Marya. That was true as well. "I'm just surprised you don't spend more time in town. You know I wouldn't mind. I remember when you two and Bill Woods were as thick as thieves."

He smiled at the memories. "Jack wasn't

even walking the last time we were in cahoots like that."

"Was it really so long ago?" she asked carelessly.

"Was what so long ago?" asked Jack. He hefted a small, solid paper-wrapped package in his hands before lobbing it underarm towards Elliot. "Hi, Da."

"How was your day?"

"I got a good discount on the salt," said Jack.

"How come?" asked Elliot.

"They wanted Ma's pies for the Seer. Paid extra for them. No one else got any. I've even brought orders back with me. Should be able to use all the apples and plums we can't store."

Elliot was proud of his son, but winced at the thought of Jack's real reason for being so late back. He was determined not to bring it up until Jack did; he wasn't going to start another argument he knew he'd lose.

"Well done." He paused, taking a chunk of bread from the side. The feel of the crust was rough under his fingertips, like birch bark. He took a bite. "So who else was in town today?" He heard Marya sigh and couldn't decide if it was because he was talking with his mouth full or that he was so ham-fisted with his son.

"Everyone," said Jack. "Dyson and Clark say hello, as does Elwyn Cooper. Wondered if we'd be celebrating harvest with them at the festival hall. I said of course we would."

"I didn't think that dancing was your sort of thing," said Elliot.

Jack blushed.

"Ah. I see," said his father. "Anna-lea?"

"Elliot, don't be so bad to the boy!" said Marya, her voice skipping playfully through the room; she wanted to know if Jack was sweet for her as much as Elliot.

Jack took a chunk of bread for himself without saying anything.

"Don't you go filling yourself up."

"Got myself a new book," said Jack, sitting carelessly on a stool by the kitchen table.

"Did you? From Riculf?" asked Elliot.

Jack suddenly looked embarrassed. "No," was all he said.

"No?"

"No."

"So who was it gave you the book?" asked Elliot. Marya had come around the table to stand next to her husband.

Jack looked distinctly uncomfortable, as if hed stumbled upon a bear at the beginning of spring and was wondering to himself if he could get away without being mauled.

"Nick," he said eventually, voice taut.

"I don't know the name," said Elliot as casually as he could manage, realising they were sailing deep waters.

"He came with the Seer," said Jack. "He's Unwin's assistant."

"Unwin's assistant."

"Yeah," said Jack, warming to his subject. "They travel together everywhere, Nick comes from more than two hundred miles away, a small village near a town I haven't even heard of." He laughed, remembering. "He said that they're on the edge of the empire, that he's seen Scarroe traders, that they've travelled with a caravan of Guardians." His eyes glittered with the glamour of another man's glory. "The book comes from Ashan. I didn't believe him when he pulled this dusty brown square from a sack cloth bag, but Unwin claimed the truth of it."

He waved his hands in the air, tracing out the interior of the book. "It has two columns on most pages, one with our letters and another in Ashan. Often, written in the margins, are Scarroe notes commenting on what's being said." He fixed Elliot with an ecstatic gaze. "Dad, there are maps."

Elliot had heard enough. With a wrench, he managed to steer the conversation away from what the boy had received from the Seer's mouth. If Jack was anything other than happy, it was because the Seer had given him the destiny he was looking for. Elliot couldn't bear to hear the words from his son's lips, to see that face tell how he would be going to war and ending the lives of others.

Elliot left the kitchen after supper. He took the bag of salt and nails with him. After kissing Marya goodnight, he made it clear he wouldn't be back.

#

"He didn't ask," said Jack, after his father had gone and they'd finished the washing up. "I was holding myself together to answer him, tell him what Unwin said was my road. I don't understand." He put the dishcloth on top of the bread oven to dry. "He's been riding my ass all week, telling me how the Seer doesn't know everything, how I shouldn't wish for a destiny of killing people for the Emperor." He shook his head. "This morning he could barely say a civil thing to me."

He stood in silence, waiting for his mother to answer. Marya let the quiet fill the room, hoping he might draw his own conclusions while she peeled some apples for filling more pies.

"Ma," asked Jack plaintively, "do you want to know?"

She already knew the answer, and couldn't feel disappointed her son didn't understand – he was still half a child, even if he had a man's body.

"What did the Seer say?" she asked.

Jack took a gasping breath, his heart burning. "He said my road was to go to war. He said kingdoms would rise and fall while I stood on the battlefield. He saw a banner with a boar on it." He paced across the kitchen, his nervousness taking control of his legs. "That's Pickton's banner. Has to be."

"Was that all?" she asked, hoping it was, that they had room to argue about meaning, about interpretation. It wouldn't change the inevitable but she vainly clung to the possibility it would delay his departure another few days.

"I thought Unwin would tell me to stay here and grow grain," he smiled sheepishly.

"We hoped that. Your father tried to hope it. He's known since the day you were born that you'd want this." There were sudden tears in her eyes, brimming over like melt water. She couldn't ask him to stay, there was no force in the world that would make her ask that.

He was pleased that his hours practising spear work and swordplay – hidden out of sight of the workers, in the barn or down in the woods – would see the light of day. Of all his most treasured possessions, his duelling manuals were the most precious. Jack was glad then, as he felt a weight lift from his shoulders, that his parents had never realised he had taught himself the art of war.

He held his mother, felt sorry for her, that her world was so small, that she was satisfied with baking and with horses, cows and pigs. He felt peace that she was content to let him be. He had prepared himself to resist her if she asked him to stay. It was easier with his da: they could exchange anger and energy, then it would be done, their words calm and respectful again. On those few times he had argued with Marya, her words and the hurt he caused her lingered in his bones, like bruises that couldn't be rubbed better.

Marya pushed herself away from him to look up at the son whose absence she could already feel aching, like someone had scooped out her heart to see if she could live without it. "Please, Jack, speak with your father tomorrow. Find him before you leave. Say goodbye."

He could feel her sadness tugging at the edges of his soul, but he decided he had to be strong, to resist understanding what she felt, so he pictured a rock around which clouds split as they blew over, rebuffing the urge to empathise. "Of course, Ma," he said quietly, over the top of her head.

#

Elliot was up before the cockerel, all but fleeing the house while it was still dark. He arrived at the cottages he had built for his workmen, to find them already eating breakfast. He could taste hot, fatty bacon in the air, cutting through the crisp dryness of the morning.

Together they finished the boundary work he'd started the day before, using sledgehammers to drive those stakes into the ground that needed a deeper pile than he could give them on their own.

Elliot was the freeholder and they were his men, but he thought they got along okay. But on this day, he found he couldn't bear their joshing and laughter as they worked. After barking at them once too often for nothing more than being happy, he sent them off on tasks across his land, leaving him to finish up cleaning the stream under the bridge by himself.

Their unofficial leader, a thin rake of a man called Jacob, knew Elliot's son had been in town the day before and settled any resentment the men felt for their unjust treatment at the hands of a man they'd thought fair.

"He's losing his only child today. Which of you would fare any better if it were you?" he asked pointedly. None would meet his gaze.

#

It was lunchtime before he was found by Jack. He'd found himself a spot in one of the high fields from where he could look down into the valley towards Shatterborough and watch the heat of the day settle lazily over the land. Birdcall barely stirred the air, and the silence comforted him.

Jack approached from the other direction and Elliot decided he would do him the kindness of not watching him build up the courage to talk to his father. His son approached like a scarecrow imperfectly given life.

He's already got his pack on, thought Elliot sadly; he's come to say goodbye. His chest felt heavy, like someone was pressing down on him with both hands.

"Dad," said Elliot to his back.

"Jack. Oughtn't you be down with Wilson checking on the mares?"

"No, Da. No."

There was a pause. Here it comes, thought Elliot.

"Why'd you never leave?"

Elliot turned to look at his son in surprise. "What do you mean?"

"Why'd you stay here, in Shatterborough?"

"It's what the seer said would happen," said Elliot, the words acrid on his tongue.

Jack nodded to himself, as if that was what he expected to hear. "It's not true though, is it?" he said calmly, watching for his father's response.

"Isn't it?" asked Elliot.

"Unwin asked after you. He asked if you were still here, out on the farm."

"Did he say you could call him by his name?" asked Elliot.

"He did," said Jack. "Said I should, on account of what you did for him when you were both my age."

"What did he tell you I did for him?"

Jack answered, his voice a thin reed of disbelief, "That you saved his life a dozen times in the War of the Three Rivers. He said you were one of the finest soldiers he ever fought for. He said you were a colonel, that you led from the front and that your strategies turned the tide of the war."

Elliot eyed his son quietly. "That what he said, was it?"

"He said you were caught at the end of the war, that you and a hundred other men were held captive in a war camp for two months, and if it wasn't for you, less than half of those you brought out with you would have lived."

Elliot's ears were filled with the sound of guards beating his men, shouting at them, killing them. He remembered the touch of the brand, the edge of the scalpel. He closed his eyes and sucked air in through his nose. Calmed himself.

"Yet still a full fifty of my men died in that pit. Men who trusted me to look after them. The Emperor gave me medals enough to hide my chest, but I couldn't stay, Jack. I couldn't fight any longer."

For want of something to do with his hands, he crossed his arms over his breast. "There is no glory in death."

"It's stupid, Da. You didn't tell me any of this. I always thought –' He hesitated.

"Did you?" asked Elliot.

"I wondered if you had any courage; that when the Seer told you to stay here you were happy to."

"I *am* happy, Jack," said Elliot. "Happy as any man has a right to be. There's peace here, the earth is good to us and the people are kind. What more can a man ask for, except reward for the toil of his hands?"

"The Seer never told you to stay here. You aren't from here."

"This is my home," said Elliot.

"Wasn't always. Unwin said you came from where he was born. That you grew up knowing only the Emperor's city."

"We don't have to look to the past to realise who we are. We don't have to jump at our destiny because someone shows us the end of the journey. There's time enough."

Jack shook his head. "Are we noble? I asked Unwin how you could be an officer. I didn't believe him, I said only nobles could serve the Emperor as more than infantry."

"What did the Seer say?" asked Elliot.

"He said it wasn't for him to tell me about who you were."

"Well, he was right about that, at least."

Jack stood in silence, accusingly. Elliot was utterly alien to him. "You know why I have to go, then. Is that why you didn't walk to me about it yesterday?"

Elliot didn't know what to say. He wanted Jack to know that his son was as obvious as an aroused bull. He wanted to tell him that every young man he'd ever known thought they understood what there was to know, how in truth they couldn't even conceive of things they didn't imagine. He could see the hope, the passion and satisfaction in Jack's face, the joy in getting his destiny now. Elliot wanted to shout at him, to grab and shake, to say, "Stop being so stupid, the world is full of blood that's too easily spilt and of lives ruined because we didn't try to *think*."

Instead he said, "I didn't want to argue."

"When I was a kid, you told me your scars came from being mauled by a big cat."

"Where are you going?" asked Elliot.

"Stop it, Dad," shouted Jack. "Stop pushing at me."

Elliot blinked away tears as he turned away.

"Tell me what happened, why did you give up your destiny to come here and farm? Tell me why you don't want me to leave and follow in your footsteps!" He thrust his arms into the air, fingers outstretched as if he were in religious ecstasy. "Unwin said you are the best of men. Why can't you be happy that I want to be like you? Why hide who you are from everyone here?" Jack stood, confusion in his eyes and a deep pleading anger in his voice. "Unwin wanted to come and see you. He sounded like the proudest man in Shatterborough when he heard we were prospering."

"Was he surprised no one knew where I came from?" asked Elliot.

Jack stopped, silent for a moment, realising for the first time that there was more than he understood. "I don't know."

His father felt like laughing, but expected it would die in his throat; instead he sighed. "Unwin's destiny was to be a Seer. He and I both had our paths read for us on the same day by the same woman. We stood in line at the entrance to the

Emperor's court – outside, of course, neither of us were that special." His mind took him back to that day. "It was raining like you wouldn't believe, as if someone had turned a tap on in the sky and left it running. Unwin's ma had brought the only umbrella, so we huddled beneath it like drowned kittens."

Jack listened in silence, wanting to speak but not wanting his father to stop.

"My father was still a general, although we'd been at peace for a decade, so he spent most of his time at court, or at military balls; at least, that was how it seemed at the time. I was lucky, we spent time playing in the palace gardens, running free and hiding from our tutors.

"The expectation from everyone was I'd follow in my father's footsteps. I had been to the military academy and played their war games since the time I could walk." He unconsciously whistled a sour note as he relived what was to come. "I eventually got called in by the Emperor's own Seer; my parents – your grandparents – were standing off to the side looking so proud of me. The Seer grabbed my chin, turned my head one way then another and said, in a voice one note away from a shout, "Farmer." The room stayed silent, but the shock on people's faces has stayed with me all this time. My own father couldn't speak to me; he didn't talk to me for a week, so ashamed he was of me. By then, I'd decided to find destiny and kick it in the teeth.

"My father decided to console me. Really he was consoling himself, that his first son would be called to a commoner's life rather than a soldier's, or even a mage's. We haven't spoken since that day." He couldn't bring himself to look at Jack. "I joined a legion that was leaving for a tour on the edge of the Empire, and damn me if I didn't find Unwin sneaking off to do the same thing."

"Did you know the Emperor's son before he died?" asked Jack, who was struggling to put it all together.

"I did," said Elliot, "and so do you. Unwin wasn't named for the Emperor's lost son, Jack. If my foretelling was shameful, then Unwin's rocked the entire world."

"Did you find destiny?"

"I'm here now, aren't I? Farming," said Elliot. "We were caught at the end of the last war. I led the men in the camp, but we never managed to escape. A daring raid led by one of the most cunning field commanders I ever met freed us. They came in under cover of a typhoon, crashing through a gate that had been blasted away by the storm. Unwin and I were as glad as privates who've survived their first engagement, because the camp's commandant had been threatening to execute us both for our refusal to stay caught. The moment our forces freed us and took me to your mother, I knew she was the one I'd grow old with." He laughed at the thought of it. "Took some time persuading her, though, she wasn't ready to leave the life."

"Sounds like you enjoyed it," said Jack.

"It was a time and a place." Elliot's voice was suddenly flat.

"So why can't you be happy for me?"

"Son." Elliot turned to Jack and put a hand on each soldier. "Unwin can tell you this himself, destiny doesn't have to be today. He and I found our lives far away from where that Seer told us to look. We realised that there's no single road to fulfilling the Creator's plan for us. I don't see why you have to run towards what will find you anyway. Wars aren't glorious. They're celebrated by those who didn't fight them to convince others to die for them."

"You *had* to become a farmer," said Jack. "This is what I *want*. If I die, then I die."

Elliot hated his son's ignorance, just then. "You have no idea what I'm saying. If I hadn't fought my destiny, hadn't decided it was the better thing to kick it in the face, then you wouldn't be here. Fate isn't what it's cracked up to be. I don't doubt Unwin's foretelling, Jack; I just wonder if you might discover that it finds you all by itself if you just give it a chance."

Jack shrugged. "So it would be okay if war came here, destroying everything in its path?"

"No,' said Elliot, "my point is this: you don't have to do what destiny tells you."

"And yet here you are," said Jack harshly.

"I'm not here because someone told me. I'm here because I chose."

"Great!" Jack threw his arms into the air. "I *want* to be a soldier. You've made it even better for me dad, I can be an officer. Unwin will witness for me even if you won't. You may have run from your fate, but I want it. Even if Unwin had said otherwise, my heart would have dreamed of this." He sighed and looked at Elliot as if from a great distance. "This is my choice."

Elliot cut his son off. "Then go."

Jack stood there a moment, his eyes pleading for something more from his father. Elliot couldn't do anything except stare, wide-eyed with loss and fury, until Jack walked away.

#

Elliot was still there an hour later. He had watched Unwin's heavy form shamble up the hill. "Jack has gone?" were his first words.

"A while ago."

"Did you try and stop him?"

"I did," said Elliot. "For all the good of it."

"He wanted to make his own choice," said Unwin.

"He wanted to run to his destiny today."

"He'll have a hard time doing that, Elliot," said Unwin happily.

"I don't understand."

"Being a soldier's not his destiny."

Elliot looked closely at his friend's chubby face, 'what do you mean?'

'I told him what he wanted to hear." He held up his hands. "Don't be angry, he couldn't stay here, you know that. The place was already too small for him."

"What is his fate?" asked Elliot curiously.

"You broke it," said Unwin. "You're still alive; Marya saved you and allowed you to become the farmer you so despised as a child. Except it wasn't your destiny to grow old." He scratched at his chin. "Nor to be a father to your son, for that matter."

"So what then?"

"That's for Jack to make for himself."

"That'll do," said Elliot, allowing himself a

faint smile. "Not bad for a farm boy."

HOME

The sun was an antique orange, shading gold through ochre, but without the warmth. It had swollen in recent millennia, until it filled the sky with its exhausted presence.

The last strategy of a condemned prisoner, thought Sim, *except the void is too vast for any star, however morbidly obese, to hope to jam the doors with its bulk on that last, long, walk.*

The plains below Sim's vantage point had been scoured of indigenous life centuries ago; no amount of bio-engineering could produce organisms that thrived when even darkest night remained a dull crimson and the last of the atmosphere's moisture had fled on solar winds to seek out new homes in new forms.

Sim stood on the edge of a high cliff. A thin shawl, coloured red by the sun, wrapped loosely around him like a runner's blanket. Sim was considered tall, if such a thought carried any meaning standing before a dying red giant. He was also slender enough that in polite company he drew remarks about 'alternative lifestyles,' about childish counter cultures petulantly adhered to. He had long learned not to listen to such pointless waffle; maybe that in itself proved the point.

Inside his bubble of powerfields, he was safe from the scorching radiation pouring from the sun. The planet on which he stood had been less fortunate, its magnetic field long overwhelmed, exposing the surface to the implacable horrors of space. The precious atmosphere that remained its last gasp; the very thinnest of heavy, inert, gases; scattered molecules of krypton clinging on in spite of the odds.

One advantage, thought Sim, was there could now be no distortion of his view. Various screens, flat and holographic, hovered in the air around him, showing streams of data, images of the sun and what remained of its system of planets, and a close-up on a family of vacuum-dwelling cetaceans feeding lazily on the bountiful energies flooding the local volume. It was a small pod: a single male, three females and two calves. There had been more pods a few decades ago but they had fled the system one by one as the star's final fate approached. Sim wondered if these had left it too late to leave – his projections certainly suggested they would be with him when the star finally went nova. He was relatively hopeful that they would be fine, although harassed, by its final convulsion. The family was certainly aware of his presence, having nosed close enough to the planet on more than one occasion for both of them to watch each other with the naked eye.

#

"You could have done so much more," his sister Verity said. "Why you choose to surrender like this, so..." She struggled to find the right phrase. "Limply! Ach, Sim, I don't understand your need to draw attention to yourself."

He remembered sighing heavily. "It's not surrendering, Verity." He steepled his fingers, elbows resting on her cherry wood dining table. "You know I could not care less about people noticing me."

She laughed; a mean, snide little snort, thought Sim. "You? *You* don't care? Sim, the day you decide to do something not to provoke comment or demonstrate just how alternative you are is the day the rest of us start hoping you actually turn up on time, or even just remember important birthdays. Your selfishness is legendary."

"Don't hold back, tell me what you really feel," he said, more angrily than he cared for.

"Don't get snippy with me now, Sim." She looked at him kindly for a moment, her eyes softening. "It's not as if we haven't been here before, is it?"

"Unless I'm mistaken, this is a first, at least for me," he said.

Verity rolled her eyes. "For goodness' sake, man, are you really going to treat me to one of your displays of diversion and avoidance? We're related by genetics and a history longer than the reign of the Roman empire." She pouted and tipped her head from side to side before imitating his voice: *"My name's Sim; I'm special. No – not like that, like this. I once started a star, so I'm better than you. You'd be wiser if you listened to my ideas about the cosmos and how civilisations should develop. If there was a God, I'd be His Gift."* She finished with a middle finger pushing along the bridge of her nose.

Sim ground his teeth. "I'm tired, Verity. Frankly I'm weary of the politics, the interference and the self-righteousness." He held up his hand as she started to laugh sardonically. "I know. I could be describing myself, but that's my point. I'm sick of what we've become."

"What have we become?" she challenged him.

Do I really have to do this? "Just who do we think we are? We used to soar among the stars. I thought we had given up planets completely. Some talked of travelling the great emptiness between galaxies. We were explorers once."

"What are we now, Sim? Tinkerers? A decrepit race of engineers?"

"I don't care anymore," said Sim wearily. "There's no one out there but us. No one against whom we can measure ourselves."

"You're leaving us because you're *lonely?*" she asked, incredulous.

Sim frowned, annoyed by her too-easy caricature of him. "No. Don't be such an arse, Verity." She mimed along with him; he ignored her. "We've lost our *vitality*. We have dwindled even as we've grown." He grasped for an example to make his point. "There was a time we would seek out new places, be they physical or informational. We tried everything to place ourselves; we constructed fabulous artefacts whose only purpose was to satisfy our curiosity. Now? We potter. We try to create life that can evolve into something like us. I worry that one day we'll destroy all we've achieved, only because we don't like the reflection it shows us. We used to *reach,* now we close our arms tightly about ourselves and are surprised when we look up and the wonder has fled."

"You've been talking to Ash," she said suspiciously.

"Don't be so insipid. I've been dwelling on our emptiness for decades. It's taken me this long to find the candidate. It will take me another year to reach it." He looked down sadly. "Once I've said goodbye to those few I care to know about my departure."

"You're serious, I suppose," she said, sitting down next to him instead of pacing the floor of the habitat.

He didn't bother to respond to that. "This used to be our home. We were like children exploring our grandparents' ramshackle old pile with its stairs that led nowhere, its cellars that seemed like they would swallow us. Now? It's as if we've grown up to discover that everything was much smaller than we remembered."

"It doesn't have to be like that," said Verity gently.

"No. It doesn't. I'm going to make sure of

that."

"For you," she said, as if confirming something in her own mind.

He shook his head, "No. For more than I can begin to plan for."

She stood up. The dim light from the dying star system gave her a wraithlike appearance, soft and delicate; otherworldly. "I was worried you thought we had committed some great wrong." She sounded relieved yet still tense, waiting for his confirmation of her hope.

Sim said nothing.

#

A soft red light – *aren't they all red now?* – blinked softly. Within the atmosphere of his fields, it was accompanied by the sound of falling water. Sim, seeing that the star was hours away from the end of its life, shook himself from his reverie and started sending the message packets he had prepared.

He felt nervous as he authorised his personal AI to fling them across the galaxy; sending them seemed to draw a line in the sand, to say he was really going through with it. He smiled. He was sure that if it came to it, he could live with the embarrassment of sending his letters and then appearing at people's homes when he should be dead. The array that would deliver his missives was half a light day distant. A deliberate strategy, so they wouldn't arrive at their recipients before he had departed properly. He didn't want people responding before he could finish up.

The first few letters were written in a flurry of indignation, score settling and bitter last words. Sim had stopped writing, left them to rest, coming back a week later to start over. He decided he wanted to be honest but not blunt, truthful but not tactless. It took longer than he anticipated; time after time he would review what he had written and get lost in memory, recalling the events that pulled him into those relationships, the circumstances that had broken them apart. Words and ideas would sit staring back at him, swimming in his vision as he tried to hold what he meant clearly in his mind. Saying goodbye for the last time was harder than he'd imagined.

The final pack of messages was far from clear of bitterness and recrimination; Sim decided he'd lived too long to care for other people's feelings quite as much as his good intentions allowed for. *Some people need a good dose of truth,* he reasoned when he read them back to himself. It would turn some people off, but they'd need a gut punch to take any real notice of what was being said to them. *There's a time for nicey-nicey and a time for a poke in the eye.*

Sim knew he was dissembling, trying to justify his own unwillingness to be honest with himself about his motivations, but figured that since he was leaving precisely because he was so bone-wrenchingly bored of the people around him, he could ride the edge of truth without being vilified for it.

There was a stark beauty in the scoured plains and dead rivers that ran like ruptured arteries across the landscape beneath him. He floated out over the edge of the escarpment where he had been perched, Buddha-like, in repose. The landscape was a carcass; the petrified forests, bones of a once-living ecology. Sim scratched the tip of his nose. He was done contemplating the ineffable mysteries of the universe. Even the great emptiness, once so full of promise when they had been planet-bound, no longer stretched as far as they thought it did. Of all the potential they had found, it remained life, human life, that eluded their grasp. Sim found it exhilarating that even if one could map neural pathways, could reconstruct simulacra of the brain in immense detail, it was impossible to fathom why some people chose sloth and others activity, why some chose friendship and others liked chocolate. He thought back to the children he had been responsible for, a few of them via natural means. Sim listed each one in turn, reminding himself of their strengths, their flaws, of his few outstanding hopes for each. When that was done, he started to drift through the ranks of his descendants. It would pass the time and allowed him, for the umpteenth time, to ensure he had written letters to all eight hundred and nine of them.

#

"Why can't you accept it?" he asked Coroll, his first son.

"How can you?" retorted Coroll. "We can go anywhere and everywhere, and yet I still cannot tell you how it feels to be you. There is no reason this makes sense."

"It makes every sense," said Sim. "You can experience what I experience, but it's recursive; as long as you know that what you're experiencing is vicarious, you'll always see it second hand, even if the feeds plug straight into your brain. The ability to reflect on the abstract is the one thing we've never found anywhere else."

"It's absurd. You make us sound special," said Coroll bitterly. "And we're anything but."

"Is it really so difficult for you to think that evolution has only thrown us up once? There are plenty of models that support the idea of humanity being so improbable it takes an entire universe to produce us."

"You know," said his son, "People once

thought planets were unimaginably rare, that we were the only species because they couldn't conceive of other life being out there and not being obviously apparent."

"No stranger than thinking God would live in the sky and have a beard," said Sim. "No stranger than believing life would be found in the basic information encoding the universe."

For his farewell, Sim travelled to find his son in one of the core worlds. The core worlds were, for all their grandeur and self-importance, recent affairs, settled in the last thousand years as humanity exhausted itself in exploring the edges of the galaxy. If humanity didn't admit its fatigue, that at least spoke to the heart of their misery. The 'long return,' as it was called afterwards, took hundreds of years and saw the mass of humanity swap living amongst the stars, on great ring worlds and habitats drifting in the interstellar void, for land beneath their feet. Sim reckoned the transition would have been more rapid if the sheer number of people wanting to make the change hadn't necessitated the terraforming of hundreds of systems in the goldilocks band of the galaxy that was stable enough for worlds to sustainably support life.

"You'd think it was me who had decided to seed himself. Not you," said Coroll. "I'm staying. We're not done yet."

"I've been through this cycle enough times to know we're repeating ourselves on a scale beyond the ability of our minds to comprehend in its completeness. What I believe is this: we're done. The oscillations of our societies are limited, a pendulum of fads and trends that come and go only to return later. I want to be something other than this system of going and return."

"I'm only thirty years younger than you, Sim," said Coroll. "I've seen the same as you. You're wrong. The rhythms you speak of are the lifeblood of humanity stopping us growing stale. Give it a few hundred years and people will seek out those mothballed rings and habitats they're so busy slating."

"Coroll. I miss belonging. I miss home." Sim looked from the balcony where they were sat, over a terraformed sea full of engineered fauna and flora, soared over by gulls and raptors undisturbed by humanity. The sun they'd chosen was a standard M3 class like the sun that played host to their home planet Earth. Its yellow light reminded him of his visits there, except the sky here was a deeper shade of blue, the ocean a crystal clear emerald. "There was a time when I knew I was part of something." He held up a cupped hand, as if holding something. "I had this sense of *rightness* when I sat with our family, I could return to places and feel a sense of peace." He dropped his hand again. "All I feel now is weariness."

"Have we offended you? Is this some great gesture to let us all know what a disappointment to you we are?"

"It's not all about you," said Sim tartly.

"Ha! No. I could never claim that crown, could I?"

"It's my decision," said Sim. "It's got nothing to do with you."

Coroll all but snarled at his father, yet remained silent. Sim waited for him to say something, nonplussed by his lack of comment. Coroll stood up from his seat, left the room and did not return. The house AI informed Sim an hour later that he could see himself out.

#

He reached the end of his count and saw the emission spectrum of the star begin to vary unpredictably. The volatility of the reactions within its heart was as expected, like the last firing of consciousness as it struggled to stay together.

Soon, he thought, and shocked himself with his own excitement. The sense of anticipation was one he had not felt for a hundred years. It touched him like a burning match to the back of the hand.

He wanted to pull away but drank it in, savoured its uncontrollable impact on his body and mind.

He slowly allowed his energy fields to pull him back to the magnetic marker he had placed in the ground at the top of the escarpment. He judged that here was the best choice among many for his experiment to be carried out. Construction would take a few minutes, but the work would be delicate enough that he had to wait until the last moment before beginning. The materials would be ripped to pieces by the solar winds in minutes.

The instant the star started its final collapse he would begin building. When built, his machine would require the energy of the star's destruction to power it, and in staying – making himself part of that process – he would die.

He was ready.

The planet was thirteen light minutes away from its sun, which gave him plenty of time once the collapse began.

#

"You won't remember, you know. In the millennia to come your molecules, your DNA, won't hold on to the idea of you, as if you were its God." Sim's friend Plato sipped at his coffee, on the far side of the galaxy. When Sim had identified his candidate star, Plato was too far away and, although a dear friend, not nearly closely related enough to warrant a separate visit. *Besides*, thought Sim, *he is mature enough not to need me to hold his hand before I leave.*

"That's hardly the point, Plato, is it?"

"I suppose not," said Plato, clearly thinking otherwise. He was sat in a room bathed in violet sunlight, surrounded by small potted plants, which covered more of his desk than paperwork. The fauna they had developed was purple and blue. "I can see why you're doing this," he said. "I'm sure it's too bizarre for others to accept as the simple truth. In some ways, Sim, I'm not surprised. You've always been a sour puss."

"I'm not trying to escape," said Sim. "I'm trying to make a change."

"I fail to see how you spreading your DNA across the galaxy in micro comets that will take millions of years to reach a fraction of that volume is 'making a change.'"

"I once started a star," began Sim,

"Oh, here we go," said Plato, cutting him off.

"My point," said Sim, sticking two fingers up at Plato and making a face, "is that I can do more than simply seed DNA. I have built an engine that will put my DNA across a number of currently uninhabited worlds and, as well as starting the process of terraforming them, will provide the key codes for kick-starting the evolution of life."

"You really do want to be God, then," said Plato flatly. "I thought you honestly objected to these cretins who are trying to re-engineer life in their own image. Are you really that much of a narcissist?"

Sim shifted uncomfortably. "Don't be absurd. I'm not trying to get *anything* except a good chance for life to come without being interfered with. I've secured permanent non-access rights for these locations" – he smiled wryly – "Even if little Sims pop out in ninety million years' time, no one will be allowed to go see them. They're on their own."

Plato's face flicked between dismay and laughter. "Trust you to choose isolation." He pursed his lips. ""How long have you been planning this?"

Sim shrugged, suddenly awkward. "A long time."

"Come on, Sim. How long? How long've you been distancing yourself from the rest of us?"

"You're not 'the rest of us,' Plato," said Sim. "You're too thoughtful to be part of that set."

Plato snorted. "Don't give me that. I've moved planetside like everyone else. I'm not so different and I'm certainly not the first original thinker. Answer the question."

Sim couldn't look his friend in the eye. "Four hundred years," he all but mumbled.

"Four centuries?"

"Give or take," said Sim, apologetically. "It's taken two hundred to find the right star – at the right stage of life – and another twelve to travel there, do my diligence and make all the preparations. The star really is in its end phase – I may have to wait a few more decades, but no longer than that; we know the cycle well enough."

"I could not wait that long doing nothing," said Plato. "An afternoon watching sport with my great-grandchildren is enough to have me climbing the walls." Plato sighed. "You are escaping, Sim. I know you can't rationalise it this way, but from an outsider's perspective, this is the very definition of checking out." Seeing Sim's expression, he hurriedly added, "I'm not judging you, my old friend, we've been friends for time past counting. It's been so long I think the memories of our friendship are mostly stored externally to my brain. I shouldn't think I need to say it, but I understand your feelings. The rest of us came down out of the sky; we're walking on the ground again. The great mass of humanity is seeking something we've lost.

"Not all of us have been aware enough to name it as you have. We miss *home*. The place of return, of peace. I think this is a fad. It might take a thousand years to work its way through our psyche, but a fad it is."

"I'd like to think my solution is unique," said Sim, with a touch of pride.

Plato shrugged. "In its own way it is." He hesitated, reaching for the right words. "Yours is a choice derivative of the context, though, and in that sense, Sim, you're just an expression of the deeper malaise."

"I agree," said Sim.

They didn't say anything for some minutes, both comfortable with the other's presence.

Eventually Plato spoke: "Excuse me if I've not completely understood your reasoning. Why are you doing this?"

"No man should outlive his home," said Sim.

"I wonder if a man should make his home where he can," said Plato thoughtfully. "Perhaps man is made for home, but our *idea* of home defines us in return."

"If that is true, then I am undefined," said Sim.

"If it's true, we are *all* undefined, Sim," said Plato.

#

Sim performed his cycle of stretches and muscle-building routines. He adjusted the fields protecting him to allow the local gravity in. He needed the resistance if he was to do anything other than wither. He reflected that such a concern was entirely pointless in light of what was to come, but habit's a hard thing to break.

As he worked through his calves and up to his thighs, he reran the models he had constructed, simulating how long it would take for the planets he was seeding to develop life of any sort. Most of those worlds would fail completely: cosmic ray bursts, comets, meteorites, unexpected solar evolution and general unforeseen calamities would do for most of them. Best guess was that nearly ninety-nine percent wouldn't even germinate. Of the remaining, a thousandth would possibly conquer worlds with slime and goo. The chances were astronomically slim, but of those, he hoped that a handful, maybe just one, would evolve further; would find conditions just right for more complex organisms. He'd done his best to screen out the worst risks, but he'd have no control over the process, which was just as he wanted it.

Kelevem's 93rd String Sonata in B# started playing, a thousand-year-old composition from five hundred light years away. The opening movement, full of passion, signalled the end of the red giant. Sim had stationed a small monitoring satellite closer to the star, which had started the music as it detected the final moments approaching. He started initiating his project, so that when the light from the sun winked out in thirteen minutes' time, he would be ready to go.

Once the star failed, the surface would collapse inwards at speeds so incredible, that even at this distance it would be visible to the naked eye. Within a short time, the outer layers of the star would slough off, ejected into space. It would take hours for the drama to play out, although the detritus would be hurtling towards him at a substantial fraction of the speed of light.

He spent the time remaining to him drifting through memories of an autumn spent on a temperate planet with his then-lover. Estel had been a peer of Kelevem's, and had forced Sim to go and listen to the woman's first performance. It had been fifty years or so since Sim had truly engaged with new music, but despite his reservations, he was utterly entranced. Kelevem caught her world's fragility – its beauty – in a soaring work that left him breathless. It was the last time he could remember feeling happy.

Estel had died, abruptly and with finality, for all the restorative powers of modern technology, in a climbing accident shortly afterwards. When Sim listened to the 93rd, he could still see her face.

The light from the star changed noticeably and Sim started the construction. The planet had no atmosphere that he could feel, but his mind filled in the gaps, giving him the sensation of a huge withdrawal, like the tide going out on a cosmic scale. The edges of the star moved as around him the land changed into a complex machine, building inwards from thirty or so metres out, crawling, centimetre by centimetre, towards Sim.

He still talked to her, even after so much time. When he was among other people, he would catch glimpses of her out of the corner of his eyes. Even Plato hadn't asked if all of this was because of her. No one else remembered her, but the extinguishing of her light left him bereft through the ages. He was trapped in the shadow of her absence.

Sim wrapped her shawl about himself, pulling it up over his shoulders one last time. In his mind there was a smell of her on the material; the idea was absurd, impossible, yet he couldn't help but remember. Plato was right: we make our homes where we are. The idea of them defines us. Estel was home for Sim, and without her delicate, infuriating, alien presence in his life, he was a bottle cast upon the waters, beaching on shore after shore but never finding home, never able to return to the one who cast him adrift.

Sim did not accept that 'consciousness' was the same as who he *was*, that when its subtle construction came to its crashing end upon death, that he would also completely stop. The science was unresolved; none could return from that realm to inform the living. If the landscapes of information they called the 'great emptiness' had taught humanity anything, it was that their ability to grasp reality directly was limited by their very biology.

The surface of the star cracked open like a lattice of threads on the shell of a boiled egg. He could feel the tendrils of his machine start to burrow painlessly into his body, deconstructing him and storing his data in seeds that would sow life on a million worlds.

It wasn't, in the end, Sim's hope that he would somehow re-emerge in some remote future, but that Estel would.

THANK YOU!

If you enjoyed this book, help others to as well!

Reviews are the most powerful weapons in a small publisher's arsenal when it comes to generating awareness of our books. We'd love to have an ad on the London Underground and a gravelly-voiced video advert playing all over the internet, but that costs money we don't (currently) have.

That's why you, our dedicated readers, are so important. Big publishing houses will have their fans, but we like to believe that ours are dedicated to reading the next book in the Oligarchy series, or catching up on the misery Sylvester likes to inflict upon Blaise Maximillian.

Honest reviews of our books mean that other readers find them. If they're full of 5* reviews, 4* reviews, 3* if you like, they will entice other readers and get them to buy. Even 1* reviews can help, as everyone likes to discuss a 1*. So if you didn't like the book, please still take the time to write an honest review.

If you did enjoy the book, we would be very grateful if you could spend just five minutes leaving a review - as short as you like - on the book's Amazon page.

Better still, tell your friends about the book as small presses tend to live or die by word of mouth.

Thank you very much, Stewart and the AR team.

www.ingramcontent.com/pod-product-compliance
Lightning Source LLC
Chambersburg PA
CBHW060423130626
46555CB00005B/2186